Out of the
Darkness

Cortland Jones

Out of the
Darkness

A Journey into the Marvelous Light

TATE PUBLISHING
AND ENTERPRISES, LLC

Published by Tate Publishing & Enterprises, LLC
127 E. Trade Center Terrace | Mustang, Oklahoma 73064 USA
1.888.361.9473 | www.tatepublishing.com

Tate Publishing is committed to excellence in the publishing industry. The company reflects the philosophy established by the founders, based on Psalm 68:11,
"The Lord gave the word and great was the company of those who published it."

Published in the United States of America

ISBN: 978-1-63418-183-9
1. Religion / Spirituality
2. Religion / General
14.11.14

CONTENTS

INTRODUCTION

ALONE IN THE DARKNESS

Then the Lord said to Moses, 'Stretch out your hand toward the sky so that the darkness will spread over Egypt—darkness that can be felt.' So Moses stretched out his hand toward the sky, and total darkness covered all Egypt for three days. No one could see anyone else or leave his place for three days. Yet all the Israelites had light in the places where they lived.

—Exodus 10:21–23 (NIV)

Yet I am not silenced by the darkness, by the thick darkness that covers my face.

—Job 23:17 (NIV)

I invite you to take this journey with me toward the discovery of a deeper understanding of the subject of salvation through faith in Jesus Christ. Through the illumination of scripture, along with personal insights revealed through childhood and adulthood experiences, I offer to those who sojourn with me through the pages of this book an opportunity to grow in the grace and truth of Jesus Christ. I aspire to build up and strengthen the faith of those who, like me, desire to grow in the grace, truth, and knowledge of Jesus Christ and the assurance of what God teaches in His word on the subject of salvation. I pray that the eyes of your heart will be illuminated with His grace and truth through the revelation of Jesus Christ conveyed in this book.

Imagine yourself a child again, alone in your bedroom. You have said your prayers and have been tucked in and kissed good night. You have exchanged *I love you*s. It is nighttime, but sleep has failed to come to you. You remain awake, unable to drift away into slumber and rest. The house is now still and eerily quiet, and your room is dark. The warm, comforting feelings you felt a moment ago have been ushered away by shadows that creep along the walls, brought to life by the imagination of your mind and your fears of the dark. You now lie in your bed, paralyzed by the haunting, echoing thought that you are not alone in your room. "Someone is watching me," you hear yourself say, and you ignore the gentle whisper within your heart that seeks to reassure you that there are no such things as ghosts or monsters.

The terror within your mind grips you like a boa constrictor squeezing the life out of its prey. You hear a deafening silence ringing in your ears. Your eyes search hopelessly within the darkness for the comfort and security of a familiar object that will release you from the sudden terror that has a stranglehold on your senses. Objects within the room appear to dance and shift within the shadows. You think to yourself that you should jump from under the covers and dash to the safety and security of your parent's embrace. The weight of anxiety and fear of the dark presses you firmly against your bed, and every movement appears to last an eternity.

You want to cry out, but the terror you feel is not only inhibiting your ability to move but is also preventing you from crying out for help. Your tongue seems to have frozen to the insides of your mouth, and you are left motionless and speechless. You cannot cry out, but in your heart you scream and shriek with a sound that is as deafening as the silence that surrounds you. Unable to alert your parents to your distress, you begin to sense that the darkness within your room is now within you. It is a darkness that you can feel. Your imagination is now in overdrive, and it has convinced you that the darkness within your room is going to hurt you.

In your anxiety, you begin to wonder if this night will ever pass. Your eyes search the darkness for some point of reference that will bring you peace. Instead, you fixate on something that only heightens and increases your fear. The doorway to your bedroom closet is open!

Without warning, you feel as if you're being pulled, against your will, into the closet. As this dark force pulls at you, your horror increases. You sense that you are outmatched in a grueling tug-of-war with the anxieties of your imagination, and the closet is winning.

Just as you are about to be consumed by your greatest fear, you realize that your tongue has loosened. What was first a silent siren of inner turmoil becomes the whimpering and mumbling of a child who is afraid of the dark. Your mutterings mimic the shrieks and cries you made when you rode the amusement park roller coaster. These sounds fall like feathers on the ears of the world outside your bedroom. You begin to notice that these meek sounds, though frail and faint, are strong enough to prevent you from being pulled through the closet doorway. With all the energy and strength you have, you summon the courage to cry aloud in the hope that you will be rescued from the fright that grips you. You shout! And then you shout even more loudly a second and a third time!

Suddenly the pull of the closet is chased away by the embrace of love! A flood of light engulfs your bedroom, shatters your fear of the darkness, and drives away the anxiety within you. You are blinded and startled by the light. Through squinting eyes, you can barely make out a face, but the soothing, gentle voice and the touch of compassion drive out worry and distress and replace them with comfort and peace. You are saved! Your weak cries of fear have brought rescue. Having the courage to cry out for help has delivered you into a loving embrace and has freed you from the anxiety of being consumed by your bedroom closet.

You rejoice, knowing you are safe, free, and loved. You don't think about the reality of facing this experience again—or the inevitability of the darkness coming back to torment you. Though you were momentarily troubled, you are tranquil in the embrace of love, trusting that you are safe and out of harm's way. Before you know it, you drift off to sleep, and when your eyes open again, it is morning, and the darkness has given way to the light of dawn.

Your fear has subsided, and the bedroom glistens with the sun's morning rays that break in through the windows. The light has transformed the ominous closet into a storage room filled with scrapbooks, toys, clothes, and shoes. You reach into your closet without hesitation to put on something to wear, intent on enjoying the day ahead of you.

If you've ever experienced the fear of being in the dark, then I am sure you can relate to the story I've invited you to envision. For some of you, this scene may be just as real today as it was when you were a child. Fear of the dark and of being consumed by my closet were among my own childhood experiences. In the process of writing this book, I reflected on those times. They remind me of my growing personal relationship with God through faith in Jesus Christ. They reflect God's eternal gift of salvation made available through Christ's death on the cross and His resurrection from the grave.

Within the pages of this book, I seek to share insights I have gained through God's unfailing, unconditional love at work in me. This is my personal memoir and testimony of how He spoke the light of salvation into the darkness of my world and began His great work of creating the life of His Son in and through me. Since receiving salvation through faith in Jesus Christ, His words in Psalm 34 and 2 Timothy have provided me an escape from the darkness of this world.

"I sought the Lord, and he answered me; he delivered me from all of my fears" (Psalm 34:4 NIV).

"For God did not give us a spirit of fear; but of power, and of love, and of a sound mind" (2 Timothy 1:7 KJV).

Seven times in Psalm 34, the author exclaimed that God would provide deliverance from troubles, fears, and afflictions. In each instance, the author declared a personal pursuit of deliverance through seeking the Lord, crying out to Him, and demonstrating reverential fear or respect toward Him.

Do you have a personal closet of darkness that you fear will consume you? It may be a closet of addiction, abuse, adultery, promiscuity, guilt, shame, grief, fear, pride, or insecurity. We all face fears of being consumed by something within us or outside of us. The Lord lovingly entreats and invites us to look to Him, to call upon His name and cry out to Him so we can be delivered from the fears, afflictions, and troubles we face in the darkness of this world. God desires to liberate us from the past sins and failures that haunt us, to provide healing from the pain that torments our souls, and to stand at our side to strengthen us. It is God's desire to equip, enable, and empower us to overcome and prevail against the troubles of life that threaten to steal our enjoyment, our prosperity, and our future hope.

God has become a great light for me in this dark world, helping me learn to overcome my personal closets of fear, abuse, abandonment, low-self esteem, isolation, and my soul's yearning to be embraced, loved, affirmed, accepted, and valued. I am growing in this relationship with God through faith in Jesus Christ. The circumstantial darkness of this world—along with the reality of the darkness within me because of sin—drives me to desire that His love will draw me ever closer to Him. In His word, God invites me to see Him as my hiding place and refuge, which shelters me from the darkness that surrounds me.

After years of longing and seeking for what my soul understood love to be, I am learning to accept and receive love from the Lord, who promises to supply all my needs and to satisfy my desires with good things. "Praise the LORD, O my soul, and forget not all his benefits—who satisfies your desires with good things so that your youth is renewed like the eagles" (Psalm 103:2, 5 NIV). At one point as a young adult in my early walk with Christ, I remember a friend saying to me that, before I became a Christian, I always looked as if I was searching for something. Amazed, I replied to him, "Was it that obvious?"

Looking back, I realize that my soul was longing for and searching for *God*, because *God is love*. I have since learned that God is the only one who can love me in the way my soul longs and needs to be loved. The pain and torment associated with growing up in a fragmented family and with being sexually abused produced feelings of abandonment and isolation. The tragedy of a failed marriage continued the cycle of family dysfunction into my adulthood, which precipitated intense feelings of loneliness, grief, and haunting thoughts of a life filled with emptiness without *love*.

Out of the Darkness describes God's personal call for me to walk away from the pain of the past, the torment of failure, sin and emptiness, and thoughts of a hopeless future. It was a call to trust Him, to believe that He has plans to help us prosper, plans for our good and not for evil, plans to give us hope and a future filled with promise and rejoicing!

"'For I know the plans I have for you,' declares the LORD, 'plans to prosper you and not to harm you, plans to give you hope and a future. Then you will call upon me and come and pray to me, and I will listen to you. You will seek me and find me when you seek me with all your heart. I will be found by you,' declares the LORD, 'and will bring you back from captivity. I will gather you from all the nations and places where I banished you,' declares the LORD, 'and will bring you back to the place from which I carried you into exile'" (Jeremiah 29:11–14 NIV).

There was a tremendous emptiness in my life, which I now realize could only be filled by the great, unfailing love of God in Christ Jesus. As an adult, I have discovered that the years of lack—the long drought when my soul was deprived of love—could never be filled by any one person. One person could never fulfill for my soul's craving for affection, affirmation, and acceptance. Marriage, family, friendship, and coworker relationships—all combined—could never satisfy a soul's continuous need for the love that God seeks to share with us and fill us with. I have learned that God wants us to know and rely on the love He has for us in Christ Jesus.

"If anyone acknowledges that Jesus is the Son of God, God lives in him and he in God. And so we know and rely on the love God has for us. God is love. Whoever lives in love lives in God, and God in him" (1 John 4:15–16 NIV).

God has prepared a special place in our hearts for Him alone, and He desires to lavish His love upon us for all eternity. Without His love in our hearts to satisfy our soul's hunger, we will spend a lifetime seeking to fill our hearts with people and things that will neither fill us nor fulfill us. Without His love, we will never overcome our personal fears, the troubles that haunt us, or the sins that torment us, weigh us down, and make it difficult to find true satisfaction, fulfillment, contentment, joy, and peace in this life.

"'Because he loves me,' declares the Lord, 'I will rescue him; I will protect him, for he acknowledges my name. He will call upon me, and I will answer him; I will be with him in trouble, I will deliver him and honor him. With long life will I satisfy him and show him my salvation'" (Psalm 91:14–16 NIV).

"He has made everything beautiful in its time. He has also set eternity in the hearts of men. I know that there is nothing better for men than to be happy and do good while they live. That everyone may eat and drink and find satisfaction in all his toil—this is the gift of God" (Ecclesiastes 3:11a, 12–13 NIV).

Perhaps part of the reason we cannot find contentment with temporal things is because eternity has been set in our hearts that we may long for the eternal things of God over the temporal things of this world. If you have a gnawing feeling of discontentment or dissatisfaction, longing for something more out of this life, you are not alone. Perhaps our desire for someone or something to fill our hearts is really God compelling us to seek and desire Him more. Have you ever wondered, *Isn't there more to life than this?* God's answer is *yes*, and that "more to life" is discovered in Him. The greater question would be, *Am I willing to seek God in order to discover what is out there for me to experience?* Ask yourself if you are seeking "more to life" through people, possessions, and positions of honor or significance.

"The thief comes only to steal and kill and destroy; I have come that they may have life, and have it to the full" (John 10:10 NIV).

"Set your mind on things above, not on earthly things. For you died, and your life is now hidden with Christ in God" (Colossians 3:2–3 NIV).

Sometimes we seek "more" because we are looking for deliverance, for relief from the calamity and adversity of life. Maybe you are experiencing a personal darkness right now that is influencing you to believe that God is angry with you, that He does not care about you, that He will never look with favor upon you, or that He has forgotten about you and will never bless you. Maybe you have a past that continues to invade your present and threatens to hold your future hostage—because you believe that forgiveness is not meant for you. Your personal darkness and the closet of your past may make you think that you are the only one who is going through such pain, and it may be hard for you to believe that there is help for you in your circumstances. Maybe life's disappointments, disillusionment, and discouragement have you entrenched in unbelief and doubt, hardened with bitterness, resentment, and anger.

The Bible is filled with accounts of people who encountered the darkness of this world that brought shame, fear, doubt, and turmoil. They needed God, as we do, to be a great light for them, to speak the light of His forgiveness, acceptance, love, mercy, and grace into their circumstances, and to bring them out of darkness into the marvelous light of His love. Faith in Jesus Christ is a personal call to salvation from the reality of the darkness of sin and this world.

"This is the message we have heard from him and declare to you: God is light; in him there is no darkness at all. If we claim to have fellowship with him yet walk in the darkness, we lie and do not live by the truth. But if we walk in the light, as he is in the light, we have fellowship with one another, and the blood of Jesus, his Son, purifies us from all sin. If we claim to be without sin, we deceive ourselves and the truth is not in us. If we confess our sins, he is faithful and just and will forgive us our sins and purify us from all unrighteousness" (1 John 1:5–9 NIV).

I close with an illustration from the life of Moses in the Old Testament book of Exodus. Moses was chosen and called by God to deliver the chosen people of Israel out of slavery in Egypt. God sent Moses to deliver the Israelites from the hand of Pharaoh and to bring them to the Promised Land of Canaan.

"The Lord said, 'I have indeed seen the misery of my people in Egypt. I have heard them crying out because of their slave drivers, and I am concerned about their suffering. So I have come down to rescue them from the hand of the Egyptians and to bring them up out of that land into a good and spacious land, a land flowing with milk and honey. So now, go. I am sending you to Pharaoh to bring my people the Israelites out of Egypt'" (Exodus 3:7–8, 10 NIV).

Overwhelmed by God's divine assignment to lead God's people into deliverance, Moses was at first reluctant to fulfill God's purpose and plan for his life. But faith prevailed, and Moses courageously confronted Pharaoh time and again, until Israel was free from oppression and hardship. This is the same Moses who committed murder when he tried to liberate a fellow Israelite from being beaten by an Egyptian. When word of his actions became public, and he realized that Pharaoh had decreed his death, Moses fled into the desert, and for *forty years* he remained isolated from and ostracized by his people.

During the forty years that Moses was secluded in the desert, hiding in fear from Pharaoh, did he encounter his own "closet of torment" for committing murder? Was there a shroud of darkness or shame hovering over Moses? Could he have felt like an outcast, ostracized by his people? At birth, Moses was hidden by his parents from death at the hands of Pharaoh. Later, he was raised in Pharaoh's household and was spared the injustice and degradation of slavery that his people endured.

But in the desert, it appeared that fate had dealt Moses an ironic blow. Perhaps he thought to himself, *Is this it? Is this all there is to life?* This is not usually the Moses we think about or hear preached about. We think it can't be the Moses who later would part the Red Sea, see God's glory revealed in Exodus 33, and personally sit with the Lord as He wrote the Ten Commandments. This Moses sounds human, ordinary, like one of us. He sounds like a man who encountered a season of darkness in his life that may very well have prepared him for what he would soon encounter as God's chosen deliverer for the Israelites. He sounds like a man whose past might have stopped others dead in their tracks, but the Bible declares that Moses persevered because he could see Him who is invisible.

Despite the humanity of Moses—and a past marked by fear, murder, and a period of isolation—God looked beyond that and spoke light into the heart of Moses. This inspired him to greatness and gave him the privilege of experiencing God's glory in a way that Moses had not thought possible. After forty years of darkness and uncertainty, Moses saw the great light of God raise him up—to help raise a nation that had been in darkness for four hundred years! Moses became a great light of hope and inspiration for man, just as God had become for Moses. Moses was destined to achieve greatness; and by faith, in God's time, he did.

Each of us is destined for greatness in our lives, and by faith, in God's time, we will see the faithfulness of God complete the good work He began in us when He created us and initiated our faith walk with Jesus Christ. Just as God came to Moses to make use of Moses for His glory, He desires to do the same with each of us. God desires to draw us into the marvelous light of His love, out of the darkness of sin and this world, so that we may, like Moses, be a great source of light in delivering others, for God's glory, from the oppression of fear, slavery to sin, and unbelief.

Like the little child rescued from the darkness of his bedroom and the fear of being consumed by his closet, God wants to pull off the blankets of sin, the past, present pain, troubles, and afflictions and embrace us with His love, kindness, and compassion. It is God's desire that we come to know Him in the way Moses and the Israelites knew Him—as the God of heaven and earth who is concerned about us, who hears our cries and sees our suffering, and who acts on our behalf to rescue us, deliver us, set us free, and bless us with an abundant life!

Jesus Christ is the Light of the World, who draws us out of darkness to God by faith. I invite you to continue this journey with me and discover God's plan, purpose, power, fulfillment, and glory—all revealed in salvation. Experience the gift of eternal life in His Son, Jesus Christ.

CHAPTER 1

DIVINE PARADOX: TREASURES OF DARKNESS

I am the man who has seen affliction by the rod of his wrath. He has driven me away and made me walk in darkness rather than light.

—Lamentations 3:1–2 (NIV)

I form the light and create darkness, I bring prosperity and create disaster; I, the LORD, do all these things.

—Isaiah 45:7 (NIV)

During the process of writing this book, I discovered that darkness should not be feared but should be embraced, or accepted, as a means of overcoming fear. The things about and within me that taunt me, trouble me, and torment me must be mastered, if I am to experience by faith the fullness of life that Christ came to give me and declared that I should have. In order for me to master something, I must be willing to face it until I conquer it.

"Who shall separate us from the love of Christ? Shall trouble or hardship or persecution or famine or nakedness or danger or sword? As it is written: 'For your sake we face death all day long;

we are considered as sheep to be slaughtered.' No, in all these things we are more than conquerors through him who loved us" (Romans 8:35–37 NIV).

In the New Testament book of Romans, the apostle Paul declared the principle of mastery ("more than a conqueror") as an act *accomplished through God*, who loves us. During the days of Adam and Eve, God addressed the principle of mastery over sin with Cain. But Cain rejected God's admonition and murdered his brother Abel out of envy and jealousy.

"Then the LORD said to Cain, 'Why are you angry? Why is your face downcast? If you do what is right, will you not be accepted? But if you do not do what is right, sin is crouching at your door; it desires to have you, but you must master it'" (Genesis 4:6–8 NIV).

Scripture is not specific as to why God favored Abel's offering over Cain's. What is evident is Cain's reaction to not experiencing God's favor. God mentioned in scripture that Cain was angry and his face was downcast, depressed, or grieved. God acknowledged that Cain needed to do right in order to be accepted. Cain was disobedient, but he was still seeking God in some way, desiring and anticipating God's favor. However, Cain was consumed by the darkness of his emotions, and he disregarded God's warning, which ultimately led to Abel's murder. Cain did not heed the light of God's instruction to master the darkness within him, which greatly influenced his actions and behavior. This led to Cain's isolation as a wanderer.

Cain, consumed by his pride and emotions, never acknowledged the murder of his brother or expressed remorse to God for his actions, even when God confronted him about his conduct. In fact, the only complaint Cain rendered was to express his displeasure with God over the severity of the consequences for his sin. He felt that he was being treated unfairly.

> Then the LORD said to Cain, "Where is your brother Abel?"
> "I don't know," he replied. "Am I my brother's keeper?" The
> LORD said, "What have you done? Listen! Your brother's

blood cries out to me from the ground. Now you are under a curse and driven from the ground, which opened its mouth to receive your brother's blood from your hand. When you work the ground, it will no longer yield its crop for you. You will be a restless wanderer on the earth." Cain said to the LORD, "My punishment is more than I can bear. Today you are driving me from the land, and I will be hidden from your presence; I will be a restless wanderer on the earth, and whoever finds me will kill me." But the LORD said to him, "Not so, if anyone kills Cain, he will suffer vengeance seven times over." Then the LORD put a mark on Cain so that no one who found him would kill him. (Genesis 4:9–15 NIV)

The darkness in Cain's world drove him to envy, jealousy, anger, depression, hatred, murder, dishonesty, indignation, and irreverence toward God. It also caused him to become isolated from God and a restless wanderer. But in spite of all the darkness that surrounded Cain, God provided His light of grace toward him by sparing his life and protecting him from his own fear of being murdered by others. God placed a mark of mercy and grace upon him that spared him from the fear of death and allowed him to experience life—even though his actions did not merit such favor from God.

In the New Testament book of Matthew, Jesus Christ declared His Father in heaven to be the one who causes the sun to rise on the evil and the good, which is what God did for Cain. Jesus Christ came into this world to spare us from a life of wandering aimlessly—with no sense of God's presence or sensitivity to Him—and from being unproductive because of the curse of sin and the anguish, emptiness, and darkness that fills the soul. Through His Son, Jesus Christ, God warns us to receive His help to master our sin and to escape the consequence of sin and the fear of death. Through the intimate presence of His Holy Spirit within us, He provides us with a mark of grace and mercy that covers and protects us. God did these things out of love for us, so that we may experience a life with meaning, purpose, and fulfillment. These qualities enable us to overcome the darkness of this world and the world within us.

Seeking to gain a better understanding of the subject of darkness led me to a review of scripture from both the Old and New Testaments. My study provided insight on the types of darkness we encounter in this world: *natural* darkness, *spiritual* darkness, and *circumstantial* darkness. I also found myself plunged into discovering my own personal darkness during this inquiry. This made for an extensive, more personal encounter with God, even as I learned about darkness. I learned more about what a personal faith walk with Christ entails. I experienced challenges that tried me and drove me to trust and rely on Him. All of this drew me closer to Him.

The journey through my personal darkness led to the discovery of His unfailing love in a more intimate, personal way. It continually reassured me that He was with me in my troubles, protecting me and preserving my life. I learned about the necessity of sincere surrender to the will of God and believing that God will fulfill what He promises and perform what He speaks in the face of misfortune, adversity, and hardship. I am learning through the encounter with darkness that God is the great Light for me. He will help me navigate through the darkness of this world. The greatest discovery and fulfillment of life is to know Him and to encounter a personal walk with Him.

Genesis 1 reveals the subject of *natural* darkness through the story of creation. Scripture reveals that darkness existed before God spoke light into existence. Light and dark were separated and given names and specific functions. Light was called "day," and darkness was called "night." Within the darkness of night, God created heavenly lights and stars, which were provided as signs to mark seasons, days, and years. Insight reveals that darkness was given a specific function within God's purposes. Through it, light became a point of reference within the darkness and a means by which darkness would be governed. Night was used as a reference point for the transition of days, seasons, and years. Within the darkness called night, light became a reference point to guide, provide direction, and help interpret the seasons of transition. Night had an appointed time of beginning and conclusion. It was always followed by the light called "day."

Day or night, God provided a means for humankind to be governed by light as a reference point for guidance, direction, and new seasons of life. At the conclusion of the fourth day, when God did this, I imagine Him smiling with great joy as He declared, "This is good!"

> In the beginning God created the heavens and the earth. Now the earth was formless and empty, darkness was over the surface of the deep, and the Spirit of God was hovering over the waters. And God said, "Let there be light," and there was light. God saw that the light was good, and he separated the light from the darkness. God called the light "day," and the darkness he called "night." And there was evening, and there was morning—the first day. And God said, "Let there be lights in the expanse of the sky to separate the day from the night, and let them serve as signs to mark seasons and days and years, and let them be lights in the expanse of the sky to give light on the earth." And it was so. God made two great lights—the greater light to govern the day and the lesser light to govern the night. He also made the stars. God set them in the expanse of the sky to give light on the earth, to govern the day and the night, and to separate light from darkness. And God saw that it was good. And there was evening, and there was morning—the fourth day. (Genesis 1:1–5, 14–19 NIV)

In the book of Exodus, we see God use the natural darkness— a plague against Pharaoh and Egypt—as part of His plan to deliver His people from captivity. Within the verses, we discover that the Egyptians *felt* the darkness. And while the plague of darkness spread over all of Egypt, God provided light for His people within that darkness.

"Then the LORD said to Moses, 'Stretch out your hand toward the sky so that darkness will spread over Egypt—darkness that can be felt.' So Moses stretched out his hand towards the sky, and total darkness covered all Egypt for three days. No one could see anyone or leave his place for three days. Yet all the Israelites had light in the places where they lived" (Exodus 10:21–23 NIV).

As children, we feared the dark that gripped us. We could sense it as something real that would harm us. We felt the darkness. But did we sense the dark itself or our fear of the dark? Is it possible that our imaginations operated in fear, making us believe we would be hurt by the dark?

How do we teach children to overcome their fear of the dark? We reassure them that there is nothing to fear. We remind them that the imagined danger does not exist. We comfort them with words of encouragement. We encourage them to encourage themselves, to fight the fear by repeating our words to them. We teach them how to change their thoughts, in tense and stressful moments, from fear and worry to something more positive and constructive. In essence, we teach children to embrace or accept the darkness as it is, to overcome it by facing it. Is this, then, how God seeks to operate with us?

While the darkness was over Egypt, the Israelites felt the presence of God through His provision of light in the midst of the darkness. It is God's desire that, while we are in the darkness of this world, we embrace Jesus Christ as the Light of the World. It enables and empowers us to stand firm against the dark forces of this world that seek to destroy us, consume us, and terrorize us. God's provision of light for the Israelites in the midst of the darkness that covered Egypt was a sign of God's eminent presence with His people. It expressed God's reassurance that He would protect and preserve them. It was also a sign of distinction, an indication that God's favor was upon His people, that they were His chosen people, and that He cared for them and would defend them against opposition.

It is one thing to know that God is present everywhere, but to know that He is present with you in your current circumstances makes it more personal. He becomes more real to you. Knowing that He *is* God, and knowing Him as *your* God, are two different realities.

A closer inspection of Genesis 1:2 helped me to gain more insight on the subject of darkness, particularly as it relates to the subject of *spiritual* darkness. Through scripture, we learn of the *natural* darkness called "night," but there is also the darkness of the world within us, which I refer to as *spiritual* darkness. I have come to know spiritual darkness as the condition of a man's inner being apart from the indwelling presence of God's Spirit through faith in Jesus Christ. This condition is depicted in scripture's account of the condition of the earth before God spoke light into existence. Study of Genesis 1:2 reveals a parallel between the condition of earth and man's inner condition before encountering the presence of the Light of the World.

"Now the earth was formless and empty, darkness was over the surface of the deep, and the Spirit of God was hovering over the waters" (Genesis 1:2 NIV).

In Isaiah 45:18, we discover God's purpose and plan for the creation of earth. God's intention for the earth is the same as His intention for those He created to populate the earth. "For this is what the LORD says—he who created the heavens, he is God; he who fashioned and made the earth, he founded it; he did not create it to be empty, but formed it to be inhabited—he says: 'I am the LORD, and there is no other'" (Isaiah 45:18 NIV).

Isaiah and Jeremiah refer to the Genesis 1:2 account of the earth being formless and empty, and each description relates to the condition of land or a city, using words or phrases like "destroyed and left without house or harbor" (Isaiah 23:1 NIV); "the ruined city lies desolate; the entrance to every house is barred" (Isaiah 24:10 NIV); "the fortified city stands desolate, an abandoned settlement, forsaken like the desert" (Isaiah 27:10 NIV); "the fortress will be abandoned, the noisy street deserted; citadel and watchtower will become a wasteland forever" (Isaiah 32:14 NIV); "God will stretch out over Edom the measuring line of chaos and the plumb line of destruction" (Isaiah 34:11b NIV); "I have not spoken in secret, from somewhere in a land of darkness; I have not said to Jacob's descendants, 'Seek me in vain.' I, the LORD, speak the truth; I declare what is right" (Isaiah 45:19 NIV); and "I looked at the earth, and it was formless and empty; and at the heavens, and their light was gone. I looked at the mountains, and they were quaking; all the hills were swaying" (Jeremiah 4:23–24 NIV).

In essence, the earth was without structure or substance. The earth was not yet in a condition that would make God declare that it was good. Then, as He hovered over the waters and made His assessment, God began to display the beauty of His holiness and the wonder of His love by declaring, "Let there be light." In the midst of the chaos, desolation, and darkness, God began to work the wonder of His greatness and majesty through the divine order of creation.

With each spoken word, God established out of the darkness what He desired, His plans and purposes for everything He created. What was once identified in scripture as formless and empty became a place of wonder, beauty, and majesty, inspired from the heart of the Master, Creator of the heavens and the earth! And everything He created, He declared to be good. God spoke into the darkness, illuminating and establishing structure and substance by the power of His word. The apostle Paul declared God to be "the God who gives life to the dead and calls things that are not as though they were" (Romans 4:17b NIV). God creates life from dead things and makes something out of what is not! This understanding of God is important to the subject of spiritual darkness.

As it was God's desire for the earth He created to be inhabited, it is His same desire for humankind to experience the intimate habitation of His presence by His Spirit. Just as God had a divine purpose and distinct function for everything in creation, including the darkness, it was also God's intention for humankind to have a divine purpose and distinct function. Isaiah 45:18 declares that "he did not create it to be empty, but formed it to be inhabited"—a reference to Genesis 1:26. Genesis 1:26–28 contains God's expressed intention for humankind, revealing His divine purpose and the distinct function intended for the way humankind would operate within creation.

> Then God said, "Let us make man in our image, in our likeness, and let them rule over the fish of the sea and the birds of the air, over the livestock, over all the earth, and over all the creatures that move along the ground." So God created man in his own image, in the image of God he created him; male and female he created them. God blessed them and said to them, "Be fruitful and increase in number; fill the earth and subdue it. Rule over the fish of the sea and the birds of the air and over every living creature that moves on the ground.'" (Genesis 1:26–28 NIV)

"The highest heavens belong to the LORD, but the earth he has given to man" (Psalm 115:16 NIV).

After the demonstration of His greatness and glory in the work of creation, God began the marvelous work of establishing a personal relationship with humankind, illustrated in His creation of Adam and Eve in the garden of Eden. Out of the darkness that filled the earth in Genesis 1:2, God brought structure and substance to the earth with the essence of His glory and goodness, and in the same way, God then created Adam and breathed into him the breath of life. God used the creative power of His spoken word—the same word by which he spoke into existence everything that is—to breathe life into Adam. In the gospel of John, God declared this breath of life as the light of men.

"The LORD God formed the man from the dust of the ground and breathed into his nostrils the breath of life, and the man became a living being" (Genesis 2:7 NIV).

"In the beginning was the Word, and the Word was with God, and the Word was God. He was with God in the beginning. Through him all things were made; without him nothing was made that has been made. In him was life, and that life was the light of men. The light shines in the darkness, but the darkness has not understood it" (John 1:1–5 NIV).

"But it is the spirit in a man, the breath of the Almighty, that gives him understanding" (Job 32:8 NIV).

"The Spirit of God has made me, the breath of the Almighty gives me life" (Job 33:4 NIV).

"If it were his intention and he withdrew his spirit and breath, all mankind would perish together and man would return to the dust" (Job 34:14–15 NIV).

"This is what God the LORD says—he who created the heavens and stretched them out, who spread out the earth and all that comes out of it, who gives breath to its people, and life to those who walk on it: 'I, the LORD, have called you in righteousness; I will take hold of your hand. I will keep you and will make you to be a covenant for the people and a light for the Gentiles, to open eyes that are blind, to free captives from prison and to release from the dungeon those who sit in darkness'" (Isaiah 42:5–7 NIV).

"From one man he made every nation of men, that they should inhabit the whole earth; and he determined the times set for them and the exact places where they should live. God did this so that men would seek him and perhaps reach out for him and find him, though he is not far from each one of us. For in him we live and move and have our being. As some of your own poets have said, 'We are his offspring'" (Acts 17:26–28 NIV).

Spiritual darkness means living in ignorance, not revering God for who He is. This includes not walking in obedience to what He intended for humankind, who was created in His image and likeness. Spiritual darkness can also refer to the passions and desires of sin, which is alive and active inside each one of us. When Adam and Eve rebelled against God and disobeyed His command in the garden of Eden, they no longer walked in the divine purpose God intended for them. They no longer reflected His image and likeness of light, the breath of life breathed into them. Disobedience plunged them into a dungeon of darkness that they would not be able to get out of on their own. Adam and Eve's act of sin revealed a greater truth, revealed in the New Testament book of Romans, about the reality of our human nature and our inability to obey God and keep His commandments.

So, my brothers, you also died to the law through the body of Christ, that you might belong to another, to him who was raised from the dead, in order that we might bear fruit to God. For when we were controlled by the sinful nature, the sinful passions aroused by the law were at work in our bodies, so that we bore fruit for death. But now, by dying to what once bound us, we have been released from the law so that we serve in the new way of the Spirit, and not in the old way of the written code. What shall we say, then? Is the law sinful? Certainly not! Indeed I would not have known what sin was except through the law. I found that the very commandment that was intended to bring life actually brought death. For sin, seizing the opportunity afforded by the commandment, deceived me, and through the commandment put me to death. Did that which is good, then, become death to me? By no means! But in order that sin might be recognized as sin, it produced death in me through what was good, so that through the commandment sin might become utterly sinful. I do not understand what I do. For what I want to do I do not do, but what I hate I do. And if I do what I do not want to do, I agree that the law is good. As it is, it is no longer I myself who do it, but it is sin living in me. I know that nothing good lives in me, that is, in my sinful nature. For I have the desire to do what is good, but I cannot carry it out. For what I do is not the good I want to do; no, the evil I do not want to do—this I keep on doing. Now if I do what I do not want to do, it is no longer I who do it, but it is sin living in me that does it. So I find this law at work: When I want to do good, evil is right there with me. For in my inner being I delight in God's law; but I see another law at work in the members of my body, waging war against the law of my mind and making me a prisoner of the law of sin at work within my members. What a wretched man I am! Who will rescue me from this body of death? Thanks be to God—through Jesus Christ our Lord! (Romans 7:4–7a, 10–11, 13, 15–25 NIV)

The apostle Paul's solution for the human dilemma of spiritual darkness is Jesus Christ! Jesus Christ, the Light of the World, is God's provision to fulfill His divine purpose for humankind and to help us accomplish the distinct function He purposed for us to accomplish when He created us in His image and likeness. Jesus Christ is the breath of life that gives light to men. He enables and empowers us to be fruitful and to bear the image of God and the likeness of His Son on earth. Beyond the initial work of salvation through confession of Christ as Lord and Savior, a follower of Christ must engage in the sanctifying work of Christ in order to master sin. God warned Cain to master sin and become more than a conqueror in the manner the apostle Paul proclaimed us to be as Christ's followers.

This point is illustrated in a conversation between Jesus and Peter in the gospel of Luke. "Simon, Simon, Satan has asked to sift you as wheat. But I have prayed for you, Simon, that your faith may not fail. And when you have turned back, strengthen your brothers" (Luke 22:31–32 niv).

In Luke 22, Jesus assembled His disciples to share in the renowned Last Supper before He faced the trial and tragedy of the crucifixion and the glory and majesty of the resurrection. In chapter 21, Jesus disclosed the signs of the end of the age and admonished His disciples with this warning: "Be careful or your hearts will be weighed down with dissipation, drunkenness and the anxieties of life, and that day will close on you unexpectedly like a trap. Be always on the watch, and pray that you may be able to escape all that is about to happen, and that you may be able to stand before the Son of Man" (Luke 21:34, 36 niv).

It is important to note that this warning relates to both spiritual darkness and circumstantial darkness, because Peter and the disciples experience both during the final days of Jesus's earthly ministry. Jesus's warning of impending calamity and His charge to be watchful and prayerful was followed, during the Last Supper, with His disclosure that He would be betrayed by one of the disciples. Right then, an argument arose among the disciples about who was the greatest. Using Himself as an example, Jesus redirected their pride to a posture of humility. He reminded them, "For who is greater, the one who is at the table or the one who serves? Is it not the one who is at the table? But I am among you as one who serves. You are those who have stood by me in my trials. And I confer on you a kingdom, just as my Father conferred one on me" (Luke 22:27–29 niv).

Jesus then called to Peter—but referred to all the disciples—and declared that Satan had requested to sift them like wheat. The sifting of wheat is the process by which grains of harvested wheat are placed in a sieve and are shuffled around and tossed in the air to separate the weeds that grow with the wheat from the grains of wheat, so that only the wheat remains. Jesus told the disciples to prepare for a season of darkness so that they might stand firm and overcome it and become a light for others. Peter responded, "Lord, I am ready to go with you to prison and to death" (Luke 22:33 NIV). Peter desired to remain loyal and faithful to Jesus, even in the face of adversity, but Peter discovered, as the apostle Paul declared, that "when I want to do good, evil is right there with me" (Romans 7:21b NIV).

In the garden of Gethsemane, Jesus asked Peter, James, and John to watch and pray with Him, but Luke's gospel says that the disciples were exhausted from sorrow and fell asleep—right after Jesus's warning to guard against being weighed down with anxiety. Pride, sorrow, anguish, betrayal, desertion—and eventually Peter's denial of knowing Jesus, invoked by the fear of persecution in being associated with Jesus—caused Peter and the disciples to encounter a darkness around them that emanated from the darkness within them. Jesus had just declared to His disciples that, if they stood with Him in His trials, He would confer a kingdom on them. But first they had to endure the season of *circumstantial* darkness that they were about to face.

Charged with the admonition to watch and pray, the disciples discovered that they were unable to do what they desired to do to remain loyal to Jesus in the face of adversity. The disciples became consumed by the darkness within them and were overwhelmed by the circumstantial darkness surrounding them—Jesus's imminent death, betrayal by one of His followers, Satan's desire to sift them, and Christ's crucifixion. Circumstantial darkness is the reality of the troubles Jesus said we would face in this life.

"But a time is coming, and has come, when you will be scattered, each to his own home. You will leave me all alone, for my Father is with me. I have told you these things, so that in me you may have peace. In this world you will have trouble. But take heart! I have overcome the world" (John 16:32–33 NIV).

After declaring salvation through acknowledgment of Jesus as Lord and Savior, a believer in Christ must engage in the sanctifying work of Christ in order to master sin and become more than a conqueror in overcoming spiritual darkness. In Luke's gospel, Jesus instructed His disciples to watch and pray so they would not fall into temptation or become weighed down with the anxieties of life, dissipation (indulgence in pleasure), or drunkenness. Jesus wanted the disciples to be observant, wise, and discerning. He wanted them to anticipate the transition of seasons and be prayerful so they would not be overwhelmed with anxiety, overtaken by sin, and rendered ineffective in their calling to be a light for others. Jesus wanted them to be able to identify the circumstances of darkness that would come. In the same way, God warned Cain that sin was crouching at the door, desiring to have him, but that he must learn to master it. Jesus told the disciples about Satan's request to sift them, but He encouraged them that their faith would not fail. When they turned back, they would strengthen others.

Just as natural darkness had a distinct function and purpose ordained by God, so also circumstantial darkness is used by God to accomplish His plans and purposes for His people and bring glory to Himself. God makes use of circumstantial darkness in the lives of those He loves to spur them on toward growth and maturity in their faith walk with Jesus Christ. He wants them to walk as Jesus did. Through this personal growth, His followers become a source of light and inspiration that motivates others on to grow in the grace and truth of Jesus Christ and in the knowledge of His will for their lives.

"I will lead the blind by ways they have not known, along unfamiliar paths I will guide them; I will turn the darkness into light before them and make the rough places smooth. These are the things I will do; I will not forsake them" (Isaiah 42:16 NIV).

> Endure hardship as discipline; God is treating you as sons. For what son is not disciplined by his father? If you are not disciplined (and everyone undergoes discipline), then you are illegitimate children and not true sons. Moreover, we have all had human fathers who disciplined us and we respected them for it. How much more should we submit to the Father of our spirits and live! Our fathers disciplined us for a little while as they thought best; but God

disciplines us for our good, that we may share in His holiness. No discipline seems pleasant at the time, but painful. Later on, however, it produces a harvest of righteousness and peace for those who have been trained by it. Therefore, strengthen your feeble arms and weak knees. Make level paths for your feet, so that the lame may not be disabled, but rather healed. (Hebrews 12:7–12 NIV)

"Consider it pure joy, my brothers, whenever you face trials of many kinds, because you know that the testing of your faith develops perseverance. Perseverance must finish its work so that you may be mature and complete, not lacking anything" (James 1:2–4 NIV).

"And we rejoice in the hope of the glory of God. Not only so, but we also rejoice in our sufferings, because we know that suffering produces perseverance, perseverance, character; and character, hope. And hope does not disappoint us, because God has poured out his love into our hearts by the Holy Spirit, whom he has given us" (Romans 5:2b–5).

A closer inspection of John's gospel, chapters 13–16, and Jesus's dialogue with His disciples helps us better understand why they were overtaken with sorrow when they entered the garden of Gethsemane and were unable to follow through with Jesus's admonition to watch and pray. In John 13, Jesus disclosed the act of betrayal that Judas was about to commit and directed him to do quickly what he intended to do. The sequence of events surrounding the betrayal concluded with a reference to the darkness known as "night." "Jesus answered, 'It is the one to whom I will give this piece of bread when I have dipped it in the dish.' Then, dipping the piece of bread, he gave it to Judas Iscariot, son of Simon. As soon as Judas took the bread, Satan entered him. 'What you are about to do, do quickly,' Jesus told him. As soon as Judas had taken the bread, he went out. And it was night" (John 13:26–27, 30 NIV).

I can just see the circumstances of darkness that began to settle within the disciples, hovering over their hearts as they tried to come to grips with this astonishing news about a betrayal among them. The One they had pledged their lives to for the past three years had just informed them that one among them would betray Him. I can just see the disillusionment that clouded their hearts and minds as they tried to make sense of what their Master had said to them. Surely each one had begun to question whether he could possibly be the betrayer. Their hearts were torn over the possibility that any one of them could do such a thing to the One they had come to love and revere. What Jesus had told them was difficult to hear; even more difficult was dealing with how they were feeling about what they had heard.

Before they could even come to terms with what they had just heard—not even grasping what had just happened in the interaction between Judas and Jesus—Jesus concluded by announcing in chapter 13 that the time for His departure had come and that the disciples would not be able to follow Him where He is going. So, not only had the subject of betrayal been broached, but it also sounded like the Lord was abandoning His disciples! "My children, I will be with you only a little longer. You will look for me, and just as I told the Jews, so I tell you now: Where I am going, you cannot come" (John 13:33 NIV).

How great was their disillusionment and disappointment at that point? Betrayal, fear of abandonment, grief, sadness, and disappointment accompanied the conversation over the Last Supper before Christ's crucifixion. John's gospel does not record the argument that broke out about who was the greatest among the disciples. I can imagine such a conversation being sparked by the alarming news of what Jesus has just disclosed to them, and in attempting to cope, their pride influenced them to boast. It may have been a way of guarding themselves against the notion of betrayal. They might also have considered this an opportunity for personal advancement when Christ asserted His authority in establishing His kingdom over Israel. In either case, the circumstances of darkness they faced aroused the darkness within them, and they did not heed Jesus's admonition to watch and pray.

Then, as they sought to grapple with the announcement of Jesus's departure, Jesus directly confronted the reality of their personal darkness by dropping a bombshell on Peter. This makes it easy for us to understand why the disciples were exhausted from sorrow.

"Simon Peter asked him, 'Lord, where are you going?' Jesus replied, 'Where I am going, you cannot follow now, but you will follow later.' Peter asked, 'Lord, why can't I follow you now? I will lay down my life for you.' Then Jesus answered, 'Will you really lay down your life for me? I tell you the truth, before the rooster crows, you will disown me three times!'" (John 13:36–38 NIV).

It was a shot to the gut that knocked the wind right out of Peter's zeal and motivation to keep fighting. How direct was *that* for speaking the truth in love? The disciples were grappling with everything their Master had just revealed to them: a disciple among them would betray Jesus, He would soon leave them, and Peter would deny even knowing Him.

How would you feel if this happened to you in the company of those you love deeply? Faced with misery and misfortune, would prayer be your first thought for resolving the situation? Have you ever faced circumstances that were so heavy and overwhelming, mentally and emotionally, that it was hard to pray? By the time they got to the garden of Gethsemane, the disciples were exhausted with sorrow.

This helps me better understand why Jesus opened John 14 by comforting His disciples: "Do not let your hearts be troubled. Trust in God; trust also in me" (John 14:1 NIV) Jesus's dialogue here offers comfort and reassurance to His disciples, helping them grasp the purpose and benefit of His departure. For the believer in Christ, God's word is the source of comfort and reassurance that helps us, in our circumstantial darkness, to overcome sorrow, fear, anxiety, disillusionment, disappointment, pride, or the temptation to deny our allegiance to Christ. Jesus instructed the disciples about the soon-to-come gift of the Holy Spirit from the Father, by whom He would inhabit humankind as earth is inhabited.

> If you love me, you will obey what I command. And I will ask the Father, and he will give you another Counselor to be with you forever—the Spirit of truth. The world cannot accept him, because it neither sees him nor knows him. But you know him, for he lives with you and will be in you. I will not leave you as orphans; I will come to you. Whoever has my commands and obeys them, he is the one who loves me. He who loves me will be loved by my Father, and I too will love him and show myself to him. If anyone loves me, he will obey my teaching. My Father will love him, and we will come to him and make our home with him. All this I have spoken while still with you. But the Counselor, the Holy Spirit, whom the Father will send in my name, will teach you all things and will remind you of everything I have said to you. You heard me say, 'I am going away and I am coming back to you. If you loved me, you would be glad that I am going to the Father, for the Father is greater than I. I have told you now before it happened, so that when it does happen you will believe. (John 14:15, 21, 23, 25–26 NIV)

"I will give them an undivided heart and put a new spirit in them; I will remove from them their heart of stone and give them a heart of flesh. Then they will follow my decrees and be careful to keep my laws. They will be my people, and I will be their God" (Ezekiel 11:19–20 NIV).

Through Cain's life and the lives of the disciples, we see that, left to ourselves, we are incapable of living out the life God calls us to through faith in Christ. This is the message of encouragement with which Jesus sought to reassure His disciples. He explained the necessity of His departure and the promise of the

Comforter—the Holy Spirit who would live in them—whom the Father would send to them after His departure. This is why God declares to those He loves that He will never leave or forsake us: because He lives in us, through faith in Christ, by way of His Holy Spirit! He is Immanuel, "God with us."

The book of Genesis records that, while Joseph was betrayed by his brothers, sold into slavery, and unjustly placed into prison, God was with him. Joseph succeeded in life despite the misery and misfortune of his circumstances. When it was time to lead God's people into the land of promise in Canaan, God told Joshua, "As I was with Moses, so I will be with you; I will never leave you nor forsake you."

God wants us to know and encounter Him as the one who is intimately present with us in the midst of the troubles we face in this life. Jesus confirmed this in His last discourse with His disciples in John's gospel. Although He told them they would not be able to follow Him where He was going, He reminded them that they would not be left alone.

"I will not leave you as orphans; I will come to you. Whoever has my commands and obeys them, he is the one who loves me. He who loves me will be loved by my Father, and I too will love him and show myself to him. If anyone loves me, he will obey my teaching. My Father will love him, and we will come to him and make our home with him" (John 14:18, 21, 23 NIV).

The events of Jesus's final days of earthly ministry with His disciples parallel the journey of faith taken by a follower of Christ, and the impact of the indwelling person, presence, and power of the Holy Spirit. Just as the disciples were invited to follow Christ during the days of His earthly ministry, so are we expected to follow Him after receiving salvation through faith in Christ. We follow Christ today by adhering to His word and applying it to our lives, which the Bible refers to as *walking in His ways* and *following in His steps*. For a period of three years, the disciples who walked with Jesus during His earthly ministry operated in the authority Christ gave them to minister and help others in need.

They witnessed the miraculous, as Christ performed miracles of healing: healing the lame, the blind, and the deaf; cleansing the leper; feeding multitudes of thousands; forgiving and restoring the sinner; and raising the dead to life!

Upon receiving salvation, we are commanded to "go and do likewise." Those who heed the voice of Christ are to lose their lives for His sake and seek to serve Him by helping others. Then we too will see the miraculous work of faith in healing and restoration. Just as the disciples were faced with circumstantial darkness in the events surrounding the Last Supper, all followers of Christ will find themselves in moments of uncertainty, filled with disappointment, disillusionment, fear, doubt, insecurity, shame, sorrow, and the temptation to deny, betray, and desert Christ and return to a lifestyle of sin.

Fortunately for the disciples—and for all of us too—the story does not end with the events of the Last Supper and the disheartening saga that unfolded in the garden of Gethsemane. There, after Judas' betrayal and Jesus's arrest, the fearful disciples deserted Jesus and left Him alone. They did not heed Christ's warning and admonition to watch and pray. They were exhausted by sorrow, and when events intensified, they were unable to endure and persevere in standing firm with Christ as He suffered.

As our example, Christ models for us the way to handle intense troubles and extreme moments of adversity—in contrast to the way the disciples handled the events from the Last Supper to Christ's crucifixion. Jesus directed them to watch and pray, and when the reality of His circumstances became more intense and difficult for Him to handle, Jesus did five specific things that provide a blueprint for handling the *circumstantial darkness* of adversity and misfortune.

In the garden of Gethsemane, (1) Jesus entered with His disciples, but He pulled three of them aside and shared his feelings about what He was facing, (2) He invited them to watch and pray with Him, (3) He went off alone to pray, (4) He prayed intensely, admitting His desire to avoid suffering but acknowledging the need for God's will to prevail, and (5) He prayed persistently. Luke's gospel records the divine intervention of an angel that came to strengthen Jesus while He was praying.

> Then Jesus went with his disciples to a place called Gethsemane, and he said to them, "Sit here while I go over there and pray." He took Peter and the two sons of Zebedee along with him, and he began to be sorrowful and troubled. Then he said to them, "My soul is overwhelmed with sorrow to the point of death. Stay here and keep watch with me." Going a little farther, he fell with his face to the ground and prayed, "My Father, if it is possible, may this cup be taken from me. Yet not as I will, but as you will." He went away a second time and prayed … So he left them and went away once more and prayed the third time, saying the same thing. (Matthew 26:36–39, 42a, 44 NIV)

"He withdrew about a stone's throw beyond them, knelt down and prayed, 'Father, if you are willing, take this cup from me; yet not my will, but yours be done.' An angel from heaven appeared to him and strengthened him. And being in anguish, he prayed more earnestly, and his sweat was like drops of blood falling to the ground" (Luke 22:41–44 NIV).

The disciples were exhausted from sorrow in the midst of their circumstantial darkness, while an angel from heaven came and strengthened Jesus in the midst of His circumstances! Jesus modeled for His disciples and for us the correct response to *circumstantial darkness*. This was in contrast to the way the disciples responded that night, but they would later be able to respond to their circumstantial darkness in the same way that Jesus had.

After Judas' betrayal, Jesus's arrest, the disciples' desertion, Peter's denial, and Christ's crucifixion, Jesus rose again! In disbelief, the disciples rejected the good news, but they had been instructed to wait in Galilee, where they would see Him (Matthew 28:10). The gospel of John describes Christ's encounter with his disciples after the resurrection. During the joyous reunion, Jesus prepared them for the gift they would soon receive, a gift that would enable them to live in loyalty to Christ, even when they fell short during the final days of His earthly ministry. Whenever they fell short, they would rise again, because they believed in the one who had risen from His own circumstantial darkness. God desires to raise others from their circumstances through their faith in Christ.

"The disciples were overjoyed when they saw the Lord. Again Jesus said, 'Peace be with you! As the Father has sent me, I am sending you.' And with that he breathed on them and said, 'Receive the Holy Spirit'" (John 20:20b–22 NIV).

Despite their shortcomings, the disciples had gone through a three-year season of preparation. They developed an intimate and personal faith walk with Christ in order to experience greater fulfillment and prosperity in being a disciple of Christ. What Jesus explained to them about the Holy Spirit in John 14 was confirmed by His intimate reunion with them in chapter 20: an event that they were going to encounter firsthand, as detailed in the book of Acts. When they stumbled from fear, pride, and spiritual and circumstantial darkness, they would be able to stand firm and overcome through the source of power and strength that Jesus had shown them in the garden of Gethsemane. In the same way, those who receive Christ today are empowered by the Holy Spirit, who helps us to live victoriously and to stand firm against the spiritual and circumstantial darkness within us and around us. We can then be a light for Christ, inspiring others to come out of darkness to be a light for others!

"But you will receive power when the Holy Spirit comes on you; and you will be my witnesses in Jerusalem, and in all Judea and Samaria, and to the ends of the earth" (Acts 1:8 NIV).

"When the day of Pentecost came they were all together in one place. Suddenly a sound like the blowing of a violent wind came from heaven and filled the whole house where they were sitting. All of them were filled with the Holy Spirit and began to speak in other tongues as the Spirit enabled them" (Acts 2:1–2, 4 NIV).

The disciples who walked with Christ experienced a moment of crisis that allowed them to see where they still lacked the ability to follow in Christ's steps. They saw that they needed His help. Even Jesus, when faced with the reality of His troubles, confided in others about how He was feeling. He asked others to pray for Him and humbled Himself through prayer to get help from God the Father. We will encounter momentary circumstances of darkness that challenge us in our faith walk with Christ. These experiences should spur us on toward a more intimate encounter with God through the person of the Holy Spirit, who will provide the strength and power to stand firm and inspire others to follow Christ.

The disciples who walked with Jesus had been invited to follow Him, and during the course of their journey, they had witnessed great and miraculous things. They had seen God at work through Christ, and now they were going to see Him at work through themselves. The greater fulfillment and prosperity they encountered was a result of having the God of the universe living inside them, enabling them to live and encounter Him in ways that they never could have experienced apart from Him.

The same disciples who had deserted Jesus in the garden of Gethsemane were arrested, beaten, and persecuted for their faith. Because of what Christ suffered for them, they did not consider themselves worthy to be considered disciples unless they suffered for Christ. In fact, the same Peter who denied that he even knew Christ eventually penned this admonition in 1 Peter 4:1–2: "Therefore since Christ suffered in his body, arm yourselves also with the same attitude, because he who suffers in his body is done with sin. As a result, he does not live the rest of his earthly life for evil human desires, but rather for the will of God."

The disciples encountered within themselves boldness, courage, resolve, fortitude, joy, compassion, and kindness—in a way that set their hearts on fire to live in a way that reflected the person, teachings, and ministry of Jesus Christ. The presence of God living within them allowed them to be distinguished and set apart as followers of Christ. Even though that distinction brought persecution and suffering, they knew a joy and peace that preserved them in the face of their most difficult hardships, because they walked with Immanuel, the God who is with us. The power of Christ's resurrection was living and active within them. This allowed them to share their possessions and to meet from home to home, which prompted believers to assemble and fellowship together and change the course of history!

> Peter replied, "Repent and be baptized, every one of you, in the name of Jesus Christ for the forgiveness of your sins. And you will receive the gift of the Holy Spirit. The promise is for you and your children and for all who are far off—for all whom the Lord our God will call." Those who accepted his message were baptized, and about three thousand were added to their number that day. They devoted themselves to the apostles' teaching and to the fellowship, to the breaking of bread and to prayer. Everyone was filled with awe, and many wonders and miraculous signs were done by the apostles. All the believers were together and had everything in common. Selling their possessions and goods, they gave to anyone as he had need. Every day they continued to meet together in the temple courts. They broke bread in their homes and ate together with glad and sincere hearts, praising God and enjoying the favor of all the people. And the Lord added to their number daily those who were being saved." (Acts 2:38–39, 41–47 NIV).

"When they saw the courage of Peter and John and realized that they were unschooled, ordinary men, they were astonished and they took note that these men had been with Jesus. Then they called them again and commanded them not to speak or teach at all in the name of Jesus. But Peter and John replied, 'Judge for yourselves whether it is right in God's sight to obey you rather than God. For we cannot help speaking about what we have seen and heard'" (Acts 4:13, 18–20 NIV).

> On their release, Peter and John went back to their own people and reported all that the chief priests and elders had said to them. When they heard this, they raised their voices together in prayer to God… "They did what your power and will had decided beforehand should happen. Now, Lord, consider their threats and enable your servants to speak your word with great boldness. Stretch out your hand to heal and perform miraculous signs and wonders through the name of your holy servant Jesus." After they prayed, the place where they were meeting was shaken. And they were all filled with the Holy Spirit and spoke the word of God boldly. (Acts 4:23–24, 28–31 NIV)

> Therefore, in the present case I advise you: Leave these men alone! Let them go! For if their purpose or activity is of human origin, it will fail. But if it is from God, you will not be able to stop these men; you will only find yourselves fighting against God. His speech persuaded them. They called the apostles in and had them flogged. Then they ordered them not to speak in the name of Jesus, and let them go. The apostles left the Sanhedrin, rejoicing because they had been counted worthy of suffering disgrace for the Name. Day after day in the temple courts and from house to house, they never stopped teaching and proclaiming the good news that Jesus is the Christ. (Acts 5:38–42 NIV)

As I have come to know Immanuel, the God who is with us, faith, coupled with life's troubles, is revealing to me the God who leads us through moments of uncertainty and uncomfortable circumstances so that we may know and rely on the love He has for us in Christ Jesus! Faith in Christ is teaching me about the intimate proximity of God in the midst of my troubles. He quiets my soul, affirms me in His love for me, and reassures me that He is with me to help me. Even when I wrestle within my soul and struggle to cope with the reality of hardship, misfortune, adversity, and tragedy that comes with life, I encounter the God who provides aid, who helps and supports me in getting through what I am going through!

"I will lead the blind by ways they have not known, along unfamiliar paths I will guide them; I will turn the darkness into light before them and make the rough places smooth. These are the things I will do; I will not forsake them" (Isaiah 42:16–17 NIV).

"'Both prophet and priest are godless; even in my temple I find their wickedness,' declares the LORD. 'Therefore their path will become slippery; they will be banished to darkness and there they will fall. I will bring disaster on them in the year they are punished,' declares the LORD" (Jeremiah 23:11–12 NIV).

Both *spiritual* and *circumstantial* darkness can bring us to places of seemingly great disappointment, disillusionment, and discouragement, with no assurance that we can press forward, push through, and persevere beyond the present moment we are faced with. But like the disciples' experience in the book of Acts, we can encounter the surpassing sufficiency, greatness, and power of God that empowers us to be bold, confident, and victorious in the face of great adversity, persecution, and injustice. Though their walk with Christ during the last days of His earthly ministry were marred by moments of betrayal, prideful boasting, desertion, denial, disillusionment, disappointment, fear of abandonment, and the tragedy of the cross, their lives on the other side of the resurrection distinguished them as followers of Christ and influenced a great spiritual revival!

It is God's desire that we encounter the same spiritual revival experienced by the disciples who walked with Jesus. God wants us to experience the rebirth, renewal, and redemptive work of the

Holy Spirit, which regenerates and empowers us to encounter the full, abundant life that Christ came to give us. God wants to raise us up with Christ and transcend the darkness within and around us to inspire others to embrace the salvation that comes by faith in Jesus Christ. He wants us to walk in the divine assignment He purposed for humankind at the beginning of time. He wants to be the great light that illuminates our hearts, enlightens our minds, and lights our souls with an unquenchable fire that fills us, stirs us, and draws us out of the darkness of this world into the marvelous light of His love!

I have walked with God long enough to witness the display of His loving power in rescuing me from the grip of depression and the disappointment of a failed marriage, separation, and divorce. I have benefitted from the sufficiency of His grace, which has covered my transgressions and enabled me to stand firm in the face of great discouragement. I have come to know intimately the demonstration of His care and concern for me.

I have seen the one who is invisible reveal Himself to me, supporting me month to month over five years as I faced imminent eviction, with no ability to resolve the problem on my own. Despite the darkness I faced and the internal night I wrestled with, I watched the greatness of the Almighty make use of me as a source of light to others through consistent, positive contributions in the workplace and in the lives of others. I was comforted to know that Immanuel was with me, despite the darkness!

In spite of my car being repossessed and the lack of a reliable work vehicle from May 2010 to March 2011, I watched God make sure that I went to work. I discovered the treasure of His intimate presence in the dark times of life, as He sustained, preserved, and protected me from the darkness within that sought to consume me. When I was displaced from an enjoyable and productive professional position, and the uncertainty made me feel uncomfortable, unstable, and disillusioned, God provided light through His word to guide me. Even in the darkness of my circumstances, my soul rested, and I found peace of mind.

"I will give you the treasures of darkness, riches stored in secret places, so that you may know that I am the LORD, the God of Israel, who summons you by name" (Isaiah 45:3 NIV).

Immanuel invites us to know Him, through faith in Jesus Christ and the indwelling person of His Holy Spirit, as the God who is with us and within us. I invite you to continue the journey to discover salvation and the treasures of darkness that await us within the pages of this book, that you may grow in the grace and truth of Jesus Christ!

CHAPTER 2

SALVATION: REDEMPTIVE LOVE IN ACTION

For God so loved the world that He gave His one and only Son, that whoever believes in him shall not perish but have eternal life."

—John 3:16 (NIV)

That if you confess with your mouth, "Jesus is Lord," and believe in your heart that God raised him from the dead, you will be saved. For it is with your heart that you believe and are justified, and it is with your mouth that you confess and are saved.

—Romans 10:9–10 (NIV)

The insights I've gained from scripture about the subject of salvation, along with my reflections from my life experiences, help me to better understand the mercy, compassion, kindness, and grace of God's love, expressed through His Son, Jesus Christ. Two recollections from my childhood, one involving my sister and the other a memory of a friend from college, reinforce lessons I've learned about salvation from reading the Bible. As I recall how their actions intervened in my life, I notice that, behind the scenes, the omniscient eye of God and His providential hand express His faithfulness to protect and provide for those He loves.

In my senior year of high school, I was enjoying what I've always felt was one of the best times in my life. School was always a place where I felt valued, accepted, and secure. It was during my senior year that I discovered something that was, for me, the zenith in peer acceptance, affirmation, and recognition. With my ability to draw and my interest in comic art, I became the author and illustrator of a cartoon comic strip for the school newspaper. I loved to draw, and more than anything I loved to draw cartoons. As I walked through the halls, people I didn't even know called me "Mighty-Mite," the name of the character I had created. It is one of the fondest and most enjoyable memories of my life. However, it was occurring at a time that was also one of the most troubling, unstable periods of my childhood.

My mom was losing her third bout with the symptoms of a nervous breakdown in what had become a four-year pattern of instability and all-too-familiar uncertainty for my family. At the time, I could not understand what I now realize were some of the consequences of my parents' failed marriage and my father's choice to abandon his family. Looking at life through the eyes of a child, I never saw my mother's problems or our circumstances as the result of divorce. I always saw my mother as a single mom trying to raise her children. My father and mother separated before I was born, but the providence of God had brought them together one last time so that I could enter human history. According to my mom's conversation with my father, my sister and I are not his children.

None of my mother's four children grew up together in the same house for any significant length of time. There were even times when my mother was not able to live with her children because of her emotional struggles. I did not realize that they were influenced by the ravages of divorce and abandonment. I could see these things happening, but without explanation or understanding, I was just left to watch. In fact, the truth didn't dawn on me until a recent conversation with my mom revealed to me that her circumstances were comparable to being homeless. The day we shared that conversation, I remember the momentary sinking feeling in my stomach as I reflected on that period of my childhood. I felt grief in knowing what life was like for our family then, and I am grateful to God for what we have persevered through and overcome. One day my mother said to me, "We are a family of overcomers." To God be the glory!

To this day, I believe that God protected me from feeling the intensity of emotions that surrounded my childhood. It would have been difficult for me to handle the emotional impact of our family dilemma—on top of remaining silent about the experience of my abuse. I have witnessed what other children experience today, and although I never truly felt the way they do, I am more sensitive to them. I refrain from saying that children and teenagers don't really have any problems, for their problems are common to what we all face: the troubles Jesus said we would have in this life. And nothing could be worse for children than to lack engaged parents or an awareness of God and faith in Christ that could help them cope or redirect their focus away from their troubles toward something meaningful and rewarding.

It is painful to see children affected by tormenting thoughts and disturbing emotions and yet be unable to cope with them. The first order of business when working with them is to speak words of encouragement that will equip them with the necessary courage to talk with their parents openly about what they are wrestling with privately. I tell them not to be like me and remain silent but to speak up and seek help. My personal childhood experiences have truly equipped and enabled me to understand and be touched by the real and legitimate problems that I see children facing today. I truly cannot comprehend where I would be today, apart from God's grace, had I felt the intensity of emotion I have seen other children trying to live with.

It was only over the past six years—after I had begun working with students and listening to them talk openly about the personal hardships surrounding their families—that I actually began to feel my own childhood circumstances. As I listened to troubled children, I could actually put words to what those emotions felt like. Helping them to identify their feelings about their circumstances actually helped me do the same for my inner child, which still wrestled with the fear of rejection and the need for affirmation and acceptance. I actually had the sense that I was being delivered from my own childhood circumstances by identifying with the emotions of my students and acknowledging to myself what it must have felt like for me in my situation. It was truly liberating!

Today I explain it as being and feeling alive for the first time. I never saw my circumstances as negative. Feelings that had been hidden away for years have resurfaced in my adulthood and tried to hinder my growth, maturity, and ability to enjoy life. If I don't manage these feelings effectively and appropriately, they threaten to steal the promise and prosperity of a full and abundant future. My family had been fractured, and only in the last two to three years have my eyes been opened to the reality that I was the product of a divorced family. For the first time, I could understand why there had been so much instability in my family as I grew up, the youngest of four children. When I was in the fourth grade, and at the end of my seventh grade year, my mother suffered from severe depression, which caused the family to be uprooted repeatedly.

In my senior year, the haunting reality of my past childhood experiences and my father's abandonment threatened to prevent me from enjoying my senior year and possibly to alter future opportunities to go to college. As my mother's sickness became worse, my sister invited me to live with her. The debilitating impact of my mother's illness hindered her from taking care of herself and paying the rent. At the time, I was not aware of these things—until I discovered an eviction notice dangling on the front of the door to our apartment after returning home from school. However, we got through the crisis every time, and life continued on. How great and good God is to not allow anything to happen to us that we can't handle. Mercifully and graciously, He will provide a way of escape so that we can bear up under our pain, momentary troubles, and temporary torment!

I remained with my sister until I graduated from college. Our mother was reunited with us and was able to see me graduate with a BFA degree in graphic design from the Corcoran School of Art in Washington, DC. My sister was married and had her first of two children when she took me into her two-bedroom apartment. Her acts of compassion, love, grace, and kindness allowed me to be the first in my family to graduate with a four-year degree. My sister looked upon my circumstances and chose to make a sacrifice that would allow me to live. She afforded me the opportunity to move ahead and become productive in life instead of remaining in the darkness of uncertainty, instability, confusion, and hopelessness. God gave His only begotten Son so that, through faith in Christ, we may live and experience His love, which upholds and uplifts us in such times.

"Before long, the world will not see me anymore, but you will see me. Because I live, you also will live. On that day you will realize that I am in my Father, and you are in me, and I am in you. Whoever has my commands and obeys them, he is the one who loves me. He who loves me will be loved by my Father, and I too will love him and show myself to him" (John 14:19–21).

Just as my sister invited me to come and live with her, providing a refuge and shelter from the unstable environment created by my mother's sickness, God invites us to live in the light of His love. Through our faith in His Son, Jesus Christ, God's invitation ensures for us an eternal refuge in heaven and a place of rest and peace as we live for Him in this world ravaged by the sickness of sin. God's love provides an anchor of hope in an unstable world tossed and driven by the influence of Satan and the consequences of sin.

My recollection of my sister's invitation helps me to explain God's plan of redemption and salvation for humankind. *Redemption*, the salvation of man, is God's divine act of love to redeem His most cherished form of creation to Himself. In the beginning, as recorded in the book of Genesis, God revealed His divine purpose for the redemption of man from his fallen nature and His plan to fulfill the promise of victory over sin, death, and Satan.

"So the Lord God said to the serpent, 'Because you have done this, I will put enmity between you and the woman, and between your offspring [seed] and hers; he will crush your head, and you will strike his heel'" (Genesis 3:14a, 15 NIV).

"He who does what is sinful is of the devil, because the devil has been sinning from the beginning. The reason the Son of God appeared was to destroy the devil's work" (1 John 3:8 NIV).

"The God of peace will soon crush Satan under your feet. The grace of our Lord Jesus be with you" (Romans 16:20 NIV).

The word *salvation*, in the Hebrew language, means "help, deliverance, victory, prosperity, or something saved." Psalm 118:5, 21 says, "In my anguish I cried to the Lord, and He answered by setting me free. I will give you thanks, for you answered me; you have become my salvation."

In Exodus 6:6, God told His servant Moses to tell His people, the Israelites, that He would deliver them from slavery in Egypt. "Therefore, say to the Israelites: 'I am the Lord, and I will bring you out from under the yoke of the Egyptians. I will free you from being slaves to them, and I will redeem you with an outstretched arm and with mighty acts of judgement.'"

In Psalm 25:22, David, the king of Israel who defeated Goliath, cried out to the Lord to deliver His people out of their troubles. "Redeem Israel, O God, from all their troubles!"

In Hosea 13:14, God told His prophet Hosea to prophecy to the Israelites, who were living a sinful, rebellious lifestyle apart from God's commands, that God would save them from the death and destruction of their sin. "I will ransom them from the power of the grave; I will redeem them from death. Where, O death, are your plagues? Where, O grave, is your destruction?" *Hosea*, by the way, means "salvation."

To *redeem*, in the Hebrew language, means "to deliver, avenge, purchase, ransom, to buy back a relative's property, to release, preserve, rescue, to deliver by any means or to sever." Essentially, redemption through God's eternal plan of salvation is His divine purpose to avenge Himself, on behalf of man, against Satan's deception of Adam and Eve in the garden of Eden, while preserving our lives from the death and destruction of sin. When we were held hostage by Satan and sin, God purchased our lives, with His Son, Jesus Christ, as the ransom.

The love God has for man is so great that He decided He would deliver humankind from the power of sin, death, and Satan's influence by any means necessary, even the death of His Son on the cross at Calvary. The power of God's love, expressed through the death and resurrection of His Son, Jesus Christ—along with the redemptive, regenerative life of His Spirit at work in and through us—severed us from the grip of sin. God desired to express His love for us through His Son so that we could experience the power of His love, the victory of the resurrection, and the prosperity of eternal life.

God expressed His love through the death and resurrection of Jesus Christ in order to rescue us from the consequences of sin: separation from God and eternal existence in hell. The purpose of Christ's death and resurrection was also to release us from a rebellious, sinful lifestyle that glorifies Satan and holds us captive in darkness and fear. This love, the power of God expressed through faith in Jesus Christ, is described in the Bible and is a gift freely given to all who are willing to receive His act of grace.

One particular experience during my college days summarizes for me the truth of God's love expressed toward me through Jesus Christ and the way His love stoops down to strengthen our hearts, lift up our heads, and make us great. Reflection and recollection of childhood memories have provided me with a wealth of understanding about why and how I've become who I am today.

It was my junior year in college at the end of the first semester, and I had just experienced the reality of having my heart broken. A relationship that had budded near the end of the summer had withered and died before Christmas, only three months later. Losing at love is never easy to get over at any age, I've discovered. The relationship didn't last long, and even when it ended, I could accept that it was for the best. My heart, however, had to shoulder the burden of the emotional load that comes from breaking up. Left with the ruins of a broken heart and a troubled soul in need of comfort, I was also faced with the reality that I had neglected my studies and was now facing the possibility of failing the first semester.

All of my classmates were gathered together, excited, nervous, and relieved about the end of the first semester and the Christmas break that was only a few hours away. All that stood in our way was the end-of-the semester review with our respective professors, to whom we had to present our completed semester work and show the outcome of our studies. One by one, we were sent into a closed classroom to be critiqued, and the tension was thick. The lighthearted mood over the much-anticipated break made the wait easier. My friend even gave me a bottle of good-tasting sparkling cider as a present while we waited our turns. When my turn came, I could not have anticipated what would happen during or after my critique.

When I went in, I wasn't really excited about my work or my efforts. To that point in my college career, my experience had been neither inspiring nor rewarding. My end-of-the-summer relationship had exposed a flaw in my personality that I, at times, still struggle with today. I can now more readily identify my struggle as having what I call "tunnel vision." I can get so focused on one thing that I lose sight of and concern for things around me—like my entire first semester of school.

My professors were disappointed in me, more so because they felt that I had talent that somehow wasn't showing up in my work. It had been that way since I had entered the Corcoran. But who wanted to hear the real reason I hadn't applied myself that semester? I responded by simply telling them that I understood how they felt and would accept whatever decisions they made. My efforts, at the time, could have brought about my termination as a student from the Corcoran School of Art.

When I exited the critique, the results must have been written all over my face. As soon as I walked out the door, everyone was in shock and disbelief about what I had been told by my professors. Friends voiced their displeasure about the possibility of me leaving, and they expressed outrage over the decision to terminate me. Although I was touched by their response and sensed my classmates' genuine concern about my well-being, this did not soothe the reality of knowing that I had put myself in that position. This further decimated the ruins of a broken heart.

The friend who had given me the gift of sparkling cider followed me out of the school as I had prepared to return home for the beginning of my Christmas break. She urged me to stay and talk, and I did. We sat in her car, and she tried to encourage me with soothing words.

It was a moment in my life that I will cherish, because her words truly spoke life into me that day. I was so moved by her compassion, her kindness, and her words that, without hesitation, I expressed my love for her. I told her that I loved her, and to this day I know why I said it and why I felt the way I did when I said it. My friend saw a young man who was lifeless, hopeless, and troubled. She saw a young man burdened by guilt and shame, consumed by the darkness of disappointment and rejection. She was concerned about someone who needed love, and she gave it. At that moment in time, she allowed *life* to speak to the *death* surrounding me in order to revive my soul and comfort my pain.

In one motion, after expressing my love for her, I reached over to her, pulled her toward me with a tremendous embrace, and kissed her passionately. That moment enabled me to live again, and we grew closer as friends. Her friendship was one of my life lessons about real love, and since then, God has opened my eyes to help me know *His* true love for me through Jesus Christ.

Just like my friend's gift of concern and compassion, God offers us His Son, Jesus Christ, as an expression of His great love for us. In the midst of our troubles, turmoil, and tragedies in this life, God comes to us, concerned and compassionate, and invites us to cast our anxieties and troubles upon Him because He cares for us. Christ laid down His life for us and said that this is the greatest love one friend could have for another. Christ offers His friendship to us to carry our burdens, comfort us in our troubles, and speak life, light, and hope into the darkness of our depression and despair. God sees us as lifeless, hopeless, and troubled with burdens of guilt and shame, surrounded by the darkness of discouragement, disappointment, and rejection. He wants us to reach out to Him and embrace Him so that He can lavish the fullness of His love upon us to revive our souls in the newness of life lived by faith in Jesus Christ. He desires for us to know that love intimately so that we may be uplifted and inspired to live for Him and to share His love with others—in spite of the tragedy and turmoil that may surround us.

"But because of His great love for us, God, who is rich in mercy, made us alive with Christ even when we were dead in transgression—it is by grace you have been saved. And God raised us up with Christ and seated us with him in the heavenly realms in Christ Jesus, in order that in the coming ages he might show the incomparable riches of his grace, expressed in his kindness to us in Christ Jesus. For it is by grace you have been saved, through faith—and this not from yourselves, it is the gift of God" (Ephesians 2:4–8 NIV).

Since that time in college, I have often experienced the great reviving power and uplifting strength of God's love that upholds, sustains, and preserves me when I am weak, weary, and worn by the troubles of life. I have witnessed God's miraculous power at work through a friend who sought to share His love with others in a way that gave life. I rejoice in knowing that God loves me enough to allow His love to revive and restore me, even when I've failed Him and have fallen short of living for Him fully as I ought to. I have lived by faith long enough to know what the apostle Paul meant when he said that *nothing can separate us from God's love*. God wants us to know and rely upon this love through Christ's redemptive work known as salvation. God wants to make the darkness light and the rough places smooth before us when we receive His Son, Jesus Christ!

With or without money, God's salvation has been with me to help me in my times of lack, need, and insufficiency. With or without the support of companionship, God's salvation has been a tremendous source of comfort, encouragement, hope, reassurance, and guidance to help me in uncertain times and unfamiliar places. With or without my ability to make things happen or get things done, God's salvation has defended me and delivered me from countless challenges and calamities that I did not think I would overcome.

God's salvation is the inspiration for this book and the driving force behind my existence and purpose in seeking to live a life of substance. Faith is the substance of things hoped for, according to Hebrews 11:1. A life of substance begins with faith. I pray that as you continue to read through the chapters of this book you will discover the substance of faith and life that will draw you closer to God to embrace His Son, Jesus Christ. I pray that the substance of faith and life found in Him and His word will fill you with the substance of His presence through His Holy Spirit to enrich you and help you grow in His love. I pray that the substance of faith and life revealed to you will cause you to share that substance with others, that they may embrace it and pass it along.

CHAPTER 3

TEMPORAL PLANS VS. AN ETERNAL PURPOSE: GOD'S PLAN FOR SALVATION

But the plans of the Lord stand firm forever, the purposes of His heart through all generations.

—Psalm 33:11 (NIV)

God is not a man that He should lie, nor a son of man, that He should change His mind. Does He speak and then not act? Does He promise and not fulfill?

—Numbers 23:19 (NIV)

When I reflect upon the theme of this chapter, I can't help but recall a lesson I learned from the Bible through the lives of Abraham, Sarah, Adam, and Eve. This is a personal experience that helps me vividly understand the wisdom of God expressed in His purposes and plans for the redemption of humankind through salvation. It also reveals to me, by contrast, the reality that His ways and thoughts are not like ours.

In the book of Genesis, chapter 12, God told Abraham (then known as Abram) that He was going to bless him and make him the father of many nations. At the time, Abraham was seventy-five years old and did not have any children. Some ten years later, Abraham was still without a child. In chapter 15, God reminded Abraham of His promise to give him a child.

In chapter 16, Abraham's wife, Sarai (later known as Sarah), told Abraham to sleep with her servant so that she could have the child that God had promised her. "The Lord has kept me from having children. Go, sleep with my maidservant; perhaps I can build a family through her" (Genesis 16:2a). Abraham listened to his wife and slept with her servant, and the servant became pregnant. This story is interesting to me, because Sarah clearly believed that God was withholding His promised blessing from her. God was talking about *birthing a nation*, but she just wanted to *build a family*.

During a Bible study with my mother and sister, I learned from Sarah's example the consequences of leaning on my own understanding. Sarah *reasoned* in her mind that remaining barren—despite God's promise—was the result of God's withholding His promise to bless her. Sarah was challenged by the passing of time, unchanged circumstances, and the same tormenting thoughts and emotions that creep into my own heart and mind to produce doubt and unbelief. My personal experience of having to wait on God and trust in His faithfulness to fulfill His promises, causes me to empathize with Sarah instead of condemning her. My own failure to remain faithful and wait patiently motivates my sympathy for her as well. It also reminds me that God knows and understands that I will sometimes falter and fail in my ability to follow through with what He requires of me. He knows that I am but dust and remembers how I was formed. Knowing this helps me to remain patient with myself when my humanity gets in the way of His divine plan and purpose to bless me.

Let's keep in mind that Abraham agreed to what Sarah requested of him. It may be because he reasoned to himself,

"Well, it has been a while, and maybe this is the way God is going to bless me with the child He promised me." Whatever Abraham was thinking, his actions compromised his ability to wait with perfect patience for God's promise to be fulfilled in his life. I thank God that His love is patient toward me, even when I can't remain patient with Him!

God's plans for our lives are exceedingly and abundantly greater than what we can even imagine—if we are willing to trust Him and allow Him to work in and through us. Needless to say, Abraham and Sarah, at the ages of one hundred and ninety, respectively, did have a child born from Sarah as God had promised. It simply took place twenty-five years after God had initially told Abraham what He was going to do. Keep in mind that it was God who came to Abraham and Sarah about the child, not the other way around. This was God's plan for them. God kept His word and invited Abraham and Sarah to participate in His plans for His people. God has plans for us that He promises to fulfill in our lives and He invites us to allow Him to fulfill His promises and perform His miracles for His people. *The process begins with salvation.*

When I came into the profession of teaching, my only goal was to make a difference in the lives of my students. I also hoped to write and illustrate children's books someday. I recall God speaking clearly to me one day, saying, "Is that all that you desire to do? I have so much more planned for you."

"For I know the plans I have for you," declares the Lord, "plans to prosper you and not to harm you, plans to give you hope and a future. Then you will call upon me and come and pray to me and I will listen to you. You will seek me and find me when you seek me with all your heart. I will be found by you," declares the Lord, "and I will bring you back from all the nations and places where I have banished you," declares the Lord, "and will bring you back to the place from which I carried you into exile." (Jeremiah 29:11–14)

I have since imagined God standing with me at a table with *my* blueprint of my life rolled out before Him. It is all about *my* plans and *my* ideas about life and success for *me.* Of course, I am feeling pretty proud and confident that these are some great plans, and I believe that God will be impressed with the ideas *I* have for *my* life. Then God rolls out *His* blueprints next to mine, turns to me, and says, "That's all you want to do? Well, *these* are the plans I have for you."

I'm sure I don't have to explain what this means to me, especially after the reminder that Sarah's plans only involved building a *family*, while God was talking about building a *nation*. The same God who intended to build a nation through Abraham and Sarah, wants to do something great for anyone who is willing to allow Him to work through them and fulfill His plans and purposes for His people.

"Now to him who is able to do immeasurably more than all we ask or imagine, according to his power that is at work within us, to him be glory in the church and in Christ Jesus throughout all generations, for ever and ever. Amen" (Ephesians 3:20).

"Beloved, I pray that all may go well with you and that you may enjoy good health, just as it is well with your soul" (3 John v. 2 NRSV).

As I began to understand the context of these two passages of scripture, I began to understand that God desired more for me than blessing me with material possessions and wealth. In fact, the context of both of these verses emphasizes a more intimate, personal expression of God's grace, power, and blessing for me, if I am willing to allow His power to work in me. I believe the greater blessing or work of God in my life is in allowing the fullness of Christ's person, or His character, to be expressed in and through me. I believe God desires for us to experience an exceeding, more abundant transformation of our character into the image and likeness of Christ.

At the beginning of His earthly ministry, Jesus began to preach about the kingdom of God. He instructed us in Matthew's gospel to seek first God's kingdom and His righteousness and not the things of this world. He emphasized the fact that our heavenly Father knows we have need of earthly things, but He challenged us not to seek after earthly things, like those who have no faith in God. Ephesians 3:20 and 3 John v. 2 both emphasize the idea that the greater work of God's power or blessing is manifested in us— as we *allow* Him to work—so that our souls may prosper. In fact, I believe that without *soul prosperity*—even if God prospers us with material blessings and good health—we will neither appreciate the prosperity God blesses us with, nor be able to maintain it with the level of reverence for God that He would desire us to have.

Soul prosperity is the transformation of the heart, mind, and will, influenced and inspired by the Word of God and His Holy Spirit to sincerely seek after God. Our hearts become loyal to God, making Him the number-one priority in our motivation for living. Our minds become renewed in consistently generating the types of thoughts that are in line with a heavenly, eternal view of life and way of living. Our strongest desire and delight becomes seeking, sincerely and willingly, to *do the will of God* in the way we live daily. Soul prosperity becomes a passionate, relentless determination to remain vigilant and persistent in action and attitude in becoming and being a Christian in all aspects of one's life. No matter what circumstances you face, no matter how trying and troubling life may become for you, and regardless of your socio-economic status in life, your *soul's* desire is to delight yourself in the Lord!

There are many in this world who have already been blessed immeasurably, more than they could have imagined, from a material perspective, but their souls are still empty, depleted and devoid of the character, *spiritual* blessing, and substance that God desires for them to have. They have not yet discovered a soul's desire to delight itself in the Lord! This is why Jesus said to His disciples that there would be no profit for someone who could gain the whole world and yet lose his soul. "Then he said to them, 'Watch out! Be on your guard against all kinds of greed; a man's life does not consist in the abundance of his possessions'" (Luke 12:15 niv).

The message of seeking after God and His kingdom is given with the understanding that the soul is in need of peace, joy, love, hope, goodness, gentleness, patience, self-control, kindness, and faithfulness, which enable and empower us to live the full, abundant life that Christ came for us to have.

Where can I go to get peace? Who can supply me with faithfulness? To whom can I turn to receive self-control? When the one I vowed to love until death parted us has drained me of the ability to love, how can I receive refreshment and replenishment to continue to give, unconditionally, when I don't feel like doing so? Whether I am at home or on the job, when I become acquainted with the stress and troubles of life, where can I turn to receive a much needed supply of patience? Where can I purchase the internal fortitude to endure until my circumstances change? Where will my help come from, when no one is available to help? When the infatuation wears off, the excitement of the latest purchase dies down, or the thrill of the moment flees, who will sustain me?

The insight that I have gained since obtaining salvation is the understanding that everyone can receive good, or blessings, from God, because God is good to everybody and loves everyone equally. But not everybody experiences the intimate expression of His grace, goodness, and blessing of the life of His Son growing in and through them, because not everybody has faith in Christ. This, to me, is the most intimate way God can express His glory, grace, and power in the life of a person. The transformation of one's character into the likeness of Christ is the greatest blessing God seeks to give to a person, because it is what

He initially intended when we were created in His likeness in the beginning.

When we really think about it, does God really need our help to do anything outside of us? God invites us to work with Him! I am learning to allow God to fulfill His purpose of growing me up in Christ, by being willing to allow His power to work in me so that His life is expressed through me. This is the greater work and blessing I can receive from God. God created me to depend on Him and to be used by Him as I learn to live through Him!

"For we are God's workmanship, created in Christ Jesus to do good works, which God prepared in advance for us to do" (Ephesians 2:10 NIV).

"Therefore, my dear friends, as you have always obeyed—not only in my presence, but now much more in my absence—continue to work out your salvation with fear and trembling, for it is God who works in you to will and to act according to his good purpose" (Philippians 2:13 NIV).

I am beginning to see that what God has intended for me in my lifetime far exceeds my plans of making a difference in the lives of my students, or writing and illustrating my own children's books. My life is a masterpiece painting in progress. I am in awe of the Master's imagination, wisdom, and power at work in my life!

There is another story in the book of Genesis about Adam and Eve that relates to this theme of "temporal plans versus eternal destiny." Satan, introduced in this story as a serpent, influenced Eve to make a hasty decision to do something on her own instead of turning to God for what she desired. This story helps me to understand God's plan for salvation and His intention to provide eternal life to all humankind.

In the beginning, Genesis 1:1, God spoke light into the darkness of this world that was without form, and from a chaotic environment, He established order. Similarly, we have experienced, on a human level, the power of God's creative genius recorded in the story of creation.

"You knit me together in my mother's womb. My frame was not hidden from You when I was made in the secret place. When I was woven together in the depths of the earth" (Psalm 139:13b, 15 NIV).

Each of our lives, like the story of creation, parallels the recorded history of God's power demonstrated in the book of Genesis. We were formed in a dark place (the womb), and at birth we were brought forth out of that darkness into the light of this world, fearfully and wonderfully made by the hands of God, the Creator of heaven and earth. Unknown to us at birth was the reality of our spiritual condition upon being born into this world. In the darkness of the womb, we did not know that, even after we were born, we would still be in the darkness of sin in this world apart from Jesus Christ. "Surely I was sinful at birth, sinful from the time my mother conceived me" (Psalm 51:5 NIV).

Outwardly, we were all born with the faces of angels, with skin as soft as silk and smiles that wooed the hearts of our proud parents. Inwardly, however, we were also born with an inherent nature that, in time, would demonstrate rebellion, hatred, discord, idolatry, jealousy, envy, strife, lust, pride, and contempt for our Creator.

The *darkness* of this world, man's inherent nature to do evil, is the result of the sin committed by Adam and Eve in the garden of Eden. Genesis 3:1–24 reveals to us the actions and consequences of Adam and Eve, providing insight and understanding as to why our world is the way it is today. In fact, the sin committed by Adam and Eve in the garden gave testament to the fact that the generations that followed Adam and Eve would no longer reflect the true nature or character of God in the earth.

"Let us make man in our image, in our likeness. So God created man in His own image, in the image of God he created him; male and female He created them" (Genesis 1:26a–27 NIV). "When God created man, he made them in the likeness of God.

When Adam had lived 130 years, he had a son in his own likeness, in his own image" (Genesis 5:1, 3 NIV).

Before the fall of man in the garden of Eden, it was God's intention that humankind bear His image and likeness in the earth. Just as our own children begin to take on our appearance and aspects of our personality, God desired that humankind reflect His image and likeness. After Adam and Eve sinned, man no longer reflected God's image or likeness, because our human nature was then regarded as *sinful*, contaminated and stained with rebellion. "The Lord saw how great man's wickedness on the earth had become, and that every inclination of the thoughts of his heart was only evil all the time" (Genesis 6:5 NIV).

Satan, the serpent in the garden of Eden, deceived Eve (Genesis 3:1–7) into believing that she would be all-knowing like God. Eve didn't realize that she and Adam had already been created in God's image and likeness. God had created them with a will, a soul, intelligence, and emotions—just as He had. He provided them a physical covering (a body of flesh) so they could live in the environment He had created for them and express His character through their actions and interactions. If God had wanted Adam and Eve to have the knowledge of good and evil, surely He would have created them with it. At the very least, Adam and Eve could have chosen to go to God to seek that information, instead of choosing to disobey God. Eve chose to listen to Satan's influence and was deceived into eating the fruit, when she saw it was good for attaining wisdom. She then gave some to Adam who was there with her.

I've learned from Adam and Eve that God never intended me to live apart from Him. God commanded Adam and Eve not to eat the fruit, and they both failed to keep the commandment *before* there was sin. The fact that Eve chose to eat the fruit demonstrates that humankind could not keep God's commandments—even when there was only one to keep! The lives of Adam and Eve teach us about our inability to live as God intended—*from the beginning*. Man has never had the ability to keep God's commandments to live His way, and without the life of His Son living inside us, we never will.

The lesson from the garden of Eden expresses to me the need for dependence upon God to live in accordance with His will. This is so that I may experience the fullness and abundance of life that He seeks for me to have in Christ Jesus. With the exception of one tree, God wanted Adam and Eve to eat freely from all that He provided, including the tree of life. How often do we focus more on what we *can't* have, instead of turning our attention and appreciation to all that we can and do have?

The Bible says that when Adam ate the fruit, his and Eve's eyes were opened, and they realized that they were naked. I'd like to think of this moment in scripture as a *blackout*. When a blackout happens, everything goes dark immediately, without warning. For a moment, we may be gripped with fear and anxiety about what to do next. We are temporarily hindered, not to mention frustrated, about not being able to proceed with whatever activity we were involved in, and we wonder, *How long will this darkness last?*

In the cool of the day, Adam and Eve's world collapsed into a void of darkness that no flashlight, lighthouse, or power station could help them out of. Adam and Eve, now fearful and afraid in their darkness, tried to hide from God in the garden, like a little child, gripped with fear, hiding under the covers. While they hid in fright, Adam and Eve tried to cover their newly discovered nakedness with a covering of leaves. Their actions, the recognition of darkness when their eyes were opened, and hearing the sound of God now walking in the garden in the cool of the day, heightened their anxiety and fear to include guilt and shame. How ironic that they were in *paradise* in the cool of the day! I'm sure, however, that it felt more like a lonely, deserted island in the dead of winter. What should have been their rejoicing and excitement at hearing the presence of the Lord in the garden, became fear of punishment from Him. They were scared because of something they had done—not something God had done to them.

What darkness in your life has you hiding in fear, under the covers of shame and guilt, away from the intimacy and love God wants to share with you? What fears in the closet of your heart pull you away from allowing God to have dominion in your heart and in your life? Psalm 112:4a (NIV) says, "Even in darkness, light dawns for the upright." Did you notice that when God came looking for Adam and Eve in the garden, He didn't judge them and condemn them for their actions? The first thing God did was call to Adam.

"But the Lord God called to the man, 'Where are you?'" (Genesis 3:9 NIV).

The Bible teaches us that God knows and sees everything, so He didn't need to address what they had done. He only wanted to see if they would confess what they had done. No matter where we are in our lives or what we get into, God comes to us, just as He did to Adam and Eve. He is looking to see if we will just admit to Him where we are and what we have done. He wants us to confess our sins to Him, so He can set us free from the dominion of darkness and the influence of Satan. God was the light for Adam and Eve in the midst of their darkness, and He is our light today. Through our faith in Jesus Christ, He helps us to come out of the darkness of this world and live in the light of His love and peace.

"If we claim to have fellowship with him yet walk in darkness, we lie and do not live by the truth. But if we walk in the light, as he is in the light, we have fellowship with one another, and the blood of Jesus, his Son, purifies us from all sin. If we confess our sins, he is faithful and just and will forgive us our sins and purify us from all unrighteousness" (1 John 1:6–7, 9 NIV).

"Therefore, there is now no condemnation for those who are in Christ Jesus" (Romans 8:1 NIV).

I believe that Adam and Eve were hiding, not necessarily from God, but from the shame and guilt of God knowing that they had done what He had told them not to do. Like the child under the covers at night, and Adam and Eve covering their nakedness with leaves, we are hiding some sin, shame, fear, lust, past failures, abuse, regrets, or unforgiveness. We are trying to cover some hurt, personality defect, family secret, disappointment, anger, prejudice, or hatred, because we don't want anyone, including God, to see us naked and exposed, feeling the shame of our indiscretion. We try to masquerade, but the weight of anxiety and the knowledge that we, His children, have fallen short of His expectations create a vice grip that is greater than our desire to be set free.

Adam and Eve covered themselves with fig leaves, but after God confronted them and they confessed their sin, *He* covered their nakedness with animal skins. God provides a covering for our transgressions so we won't have to try to hide in condemnation and fear. But we must be willing to uncover ourselves! We must be willing to come out of the darkness of our mental and emotional torment and our personal closets of the past and sincerely seek to live in the light of His forgiveness, grace, and truth!

I believe that Adam and Eve did not know that their actions would be devastating to them and eventually detrimental to the eternal preservation of humankind and every generation that followed them. Fortunately for both them and us, God's plan in creation included a plan of redemption for Adam and Eve's sin. There is a plan of salvation for everyone who accepts, believes, and confesses that Jesus Christ is Lord and who acknowledges Him as the Son of God, raised from the dead.

"So the Lord God said to the serpent, 'Because you have done this, I will put enmity between you and the woman, and between your offspring [seed] and hers; he will crush your head, and you will strike his heel'" (Genesis 3:14a, 15 NIV).

At that moment in history, God revealed to Satan His eternal plan of redemption and salvation for all men, from generation to generation, and His intentions from the beginning. God had a plan for Adam and Eve's sin! God has a solution to our problems, a plan of redemption and salvation for our mistakes, failures, and pain from the past. Basically, God told Satan that, though he may have influence to tempt us and deceive us to choose sin and rebel against God's authority, God Himself would provide His power to deliver us from our darkness in this world into the marvelous light of His love! God wants to deliver us from the dominion of darkness in this world, from sin, and from Satan's influence over us—all through the light of His word expressed in the life of His Son, Jesus Christ.

> In the beginning was the Word, and the Word was with God, and the Word was God. He was with God in the beginning. Through Him all things were made; without Him nothing was made that has been made. In him was life and that life was the light of men. The light shines in the darkness, but the darkness has not understood it. The true light that gives light to every man was coming into the world. He was in the world, and though the world was made through Him, the world did not recognize Him. Yet to all who received Him, to those who believed in His name, He gave the right to become children of God. (John 1:1–5, 9–10, 12 NIV)

The closet of my childhood meant silently enduring sexual abuse as a child and remaining quiet about my past until I was in my late twenties. I had a tremendous fear of the dark while I was growing up in my house in Washington, DC. As a child, I frequently had a disturbing, reoccurring dream of being pulled into the darkness of my closet. I remember that when I tried to scream out loud, I became conscious and realized I was dreaming. My body then became immensely tense, and it was difficult to move, even when I could hear my mind telling my body to get up.

To this day, I recall a period later in my young adult life when God told me that I had not asked for the abuse. I had not chosen for it to happen to me, so I was not to let it rule how I lived and learned to value myself. Later, at the age of twenty-eight, I testified about my experience to a group of men at a men's church retreat, sponsored by the church I currently attend, Reid Temple AME Church, where Rev. Dr. Lee P. Washington is the pastor. I shared with them that I had been the victim of sexual abuse as a child. Afterward confessing this before the men, I felt as if the emotional weight I'd carried during my childhood was lifted that night. The silence had been broken, and the darkness of my past was gone.

To this day, I know that being abused and not talking about it created a period of low self-esteem and a long period of depression due to my self-imposed silence. I believe this silence hindered my maturity into adulthood. My self-image, self-esteem, and self-confidence had been stunted, and normal development in healthy, interpersonal, peer relationships had been slowed. I was tremendously shy and spent many days being quiet and withdrawn, even in the company of others.

As a teenager, hanging out with my friends, I remained quiet, in the background, and listened to everyone else talk. Occasionally I would contribute comments and expressions, but for the most part, I remained silent. I felt safer in my silence, less vulnerable to rejection and off the radar of peers who had a newfound interest in the art of joaning, or putting people down. The less I talked, the more invisible I became, and my peers wouldn't single me out and talk about me.

However, I was never quite invisible enough. "Four-eyes" and other comments, mostly about my having to wear glasses, always hurt, but I learned to laugh it off and hide the pain. Seeds of insecurity were planted, and low self-esteem grew. From my damaged intrapersonal struggle—my conflict within—the fear of rejection motivated my sincere yet unbalanced effort to please others. My comfort, assurance, and feelings of self-worth became dependent on making others feel good and doing nice things for other people. When this was accomplished, I felt good about myself. But I had not learned how to feel good about myself simply because I was Cortland Jones.

My father abandoned my family and divorced my mother before I was born. Being the last of four children, I only have two memories of him, which were actually good ones. He visited once to take us bowling and another time for horseback riding. That was the last I remember seeing him. All this occurred before we moved from DC around 1977. I was born in 1968. I don't ever recall having hatred for my dad or a feeling of insecurity due to his absence. I even recall telling my mom one day that I couldn't say I really wished he was involved in my life. I couldn't say whether things would have been better with him, and I didn't feel as if they were worse without him. I still don't know how I came to that conclusion, but it has enabled me to live and enjoy the life I've been given, in spite of his absence and role in my growing up. His absence was not without consequences, but God's continual presence and faithfulness to take care of His chosen ones has more than made up for any lack where my father fell short.

I did not spend a lot of time with my siblings, because my two older brothers were seven and six years older than me and spent some of their childhood living with our father. My sister was four years older than I, and although I appreciated her efforts of love, attention, and involvement in my growing up, it never satisfied the growing longing to experience a whole, healthy family that spent time together. No one was aware of my abuse, so there was a darkness and pain that could never be alleviated as long as I was silent.

My darkness was the pain of feeling rejected and abandoned. I didn't want to feel unwanted. I longed for the love, acceptance, and value I believe a family should provide. My darkness was a result of years of silence, living with a secret sin that was forced upon me. For years it affected my self-esteem and caused me to cover myself, hiding who I was, how I felt about myself, and what had happened to me. It was hard to look at photographs of myself, because it usually reminded me of pain.

When I was a child, it never really dawned on me to tell anyone about my abuse. I just got up every new day, without complaints or cares. I realize now, in working with children and talking more about my past, that *numb* would be a good word to describe how I felt as a child growing up in my personal darkness. I didn't really feel anything. I just existed in my world and quietly observed the day-to-day experiences around me. The real *me* was in a coma. I felt like I was a quiet observer in the world I lived in—until one day God taught me how to speak. God taught me how to express to others who the real Cortland Jones is.

I am learning how to understand and express who I am to others and to identify the feelings I've buried for so long. I now know how to identify these feelings through listening to and helping children talk about their darkness, their pain. By listening to them, I understand how I felt as a child and how I may feel now as an adult. My deliverance has come through my faith in accepting Jesus Christ as my Lord and Savior. Learning how to share my past pain and experiences with others, as they are willing to share with me, has cultivated a ministry of love, encouragement, and support, which has stimulated growth, healing, and strength. Hope, healing, and renewal has strengthened my heart and given me balance.

My times of silence taught me to listen to others and hear the sounds of pain, the voice of God, and the yearning of a soul for something more than the moment. My abuse has taught me how to be sensitive, compassionate, and understanding of others who share that same darkness. My past has empowered me to encourage many young people, to identify with their past and present pains, and to provide them with hope, comfort, and peace by inviting them into my own past darkness and walking with them in their present darkness. When I consider my childhood experiences with fear of the dark, rejection, abuse, the numbness of growing up, abandonment, lack of confidence, low self-esteem, and insecurity, I can see what Christ has accomplished through me. Today, Romans 8:28 makes so much sense to me, and it is comforting and encouraging to hear it over and over as an adult.

"And we know that all things work together for good to them that love God, to them who are called according to His purpose" (Romans 8:28 KJV).

One day in the spring of 1993, God spoke a ray of light into my dark world through a friend, whom I affectionately referred to as "Sunshine," because she had a smile that lit up and brightened my world when I saw her. To this day, I remember the event and the words she spoke to me, but I cannot recall why we were having this conversation. What I do remember, as if it were yesterday, are these words: "I am the way, the truth and the life. No one comes to the Father except through me" (John 14:6 NIV).

Those words changed my life forever. Not long after they were spoken to me, I was invited and inspired to join Reid Temple AME Church, and I gave my life to Jesus Christ. I have not looked back since. My past helps me to understand who I am presently, and God helps me to understand who I am becoming in Christ. In light of who I was in the past, I appreciate who I am today, and I see the miracles God uses to bless the lives of many others by being willing to share my past with them.

I feel the way David felt in Psalm 27. God became my light and my salvation from the darkness of my past. He continues to deliver me from hidden places where the dominion of darkness still has influence to pull me into a place of insecurity, doubt, shame, guilt, fear, and unworthiness. God has used His word, His Spirit, the preaching of my pastor and others, and the comfort and encouragement of friends, family, and children to bring me into a marvelous light of love, appreciation, attention, acceptance, affirmation, and affection. Through these, He has lifted my head and strengthened my heart.

God spoke light into my dark world and delivered me from the fears of my closet through the saving grace of His Son, Jesus Christ. I am now living in the marvelous light of the love, counsel, and comfort He provides for His children. I am discovering the beauty, splendor, and glory of His love, written in His word. I have learned to put trust in His word and the life of His Son. I am growing in the grace and knowledge of His Son, and through His word I am learning who I am in Christ, the plans and purposes God has for me, and His uses for the gifts and abilities He's given me to serve Him in building up others as He has done for me. I am discovering talents I did not know I had. I am becoming a person I never saw myself to be!

There is a child in each of us who hides under the covers in the darkness of this world. Everybody's cover is different, but all our covers are common to one another. For some the cover is wealth, prestige, success, work, pride, fear, doubt, or shame. It could be a broken heart, emotional pain, disappointment, discouragement, or the guilt or shame of some past sin, like an abortion, divorce, or substance abuse. The pain of being rejected, abused, or abandoned may have crippled our self-esteem, leaving us feeling lonely, isolated, and unloved. We may be bound by unforgiveness, bitterness, or resentment.

Whatever your cover is, I believe God wants to allow the light of His truth and His Son to bring you out of that darkness into the marvelous light of His acceptance, love, and forgiveness through a growing, transforming faith in His Son, Jesus Christ. God does not want you to remain in the dominion of darkness. Take His hand and let Him lead you out.

I believe that Christians can still be in darkness or experience a dark time in life. We all need the transforming grace and truth of God's word and His Son to aid us in getting through what we are going through. In the next chapter, as we learn more about God's purpose in salvation, I pray that God will make the darkness light before you and give light to your eyes, to strengthen you and inspire you to greatness!

"Even in darkness, light dawns for the upright" (Psalm 112:4a NIV).

CHAPTER 4

MY FATHER AS A ROLLING STONE: GOD'S PURPOSE IN SALVATION

Here I am! I stand at the door and knock. If anyone hears my voice and opens the door, I will come in and eat with him, and he with me.

—Revelation 3:20 (NIV)

I will give you a new heart and put a new spirit in you; I will remove from you your heart of stone and give you a heart of flesh. And I will put my Spirit in you and move you to follow my decrees and be careful to keep my laws.

—Ezekiel 36:26–27

In chapter 2, we talked about God's plan of salvation. *Redemption* is a divine *act* by God to deliver the soul of man from sin, death, and Satan. *Salvation* is God's divine *plan* of love, expressed through His Son, Jesus Christ, to save us from remaining eternally separated from God, condemned to spend eternity in hell. When Adam and Eve rebelled against God's command and ate the fruit from the tree in the garden of Eden, sin entered into the world, for Satan had deceived man to disobey God.

According to 1 John 3:4–5, sin is lawlessness, and it was for this reason that Jesus came into the world. "Everyone who sins breaks the law; in fact, sin is lawlessness. But you know that he appeared so that he might take away our sins. And in him is no sin."

In Romans 5:12–19, the scriptures explain the origin of sin, sin's effects from the beginning of time to today, and the relevance of Adam's life in comparison and contrast to the life of Jesus.

> Therefore just as sin entered the world through one man, and death through sin, and in this way death came to all men, because all sinned—for before the law was given, sin was in the world. But sin is not taken into account where there is no law. Nevertheless, death reigned from the time of Adam to the time of Moses, even over those who did not sin by breaking a command, as did Adam, who was a pattern of the one to come. But the gift is not like the trespass. For if the many died by the trespass of the one man, how much more did God's grace and the gift that came by the grace of the one man, Jesus Christ, overflow to the many! Again, the gift of God is not like the result of the one man's sin: the judgment followed one sin and brought condemnation, but the gift followed many trespasses and brought justification. For if, by the trespass of the one man, death reigned through that one man, how much more will those who receive God's abundant provision of grace and of the gift of righteousness reign in life through the one man, Jesus Christ. Consequently, just as the result of one trespass was condemnation for all men, so also the result of one act of righteousness was justification that brings life for all men. For just as through the disobedience of the one man the many were made sinners, so also through the obedience of the one man the many will be made righteous. (Romans 5:12–19 NIV)

As an educator, I often use the illustration of a boulder, a steep hill, and a little village in a valley to explain to my students what can be the result of their poor choices and actions in the course of a school day and how they relate to life in general. "Imagine being at the top of a steep hill," I say to them. "Standing before you is a huge boulder, and off to the side is a sign that says, 'Danger! Please *do not* push!' Intrigued by the sign and curious about the unknown danger surrounding this rock, you want to investigate. *What possible danger could there be in pushing the boulder?* you wonder, and the idea of pushing the boulder becomes even more enticing. You choose to push it. It is only after you have set the stone in motion and watched it disappear from view that you look beyond the steep hill where you stand. You notice a little village in the valley below, directly in the path of the boulder you just pushed over.

"Immediately you are gripped with horror, anxiety, and guilt for the actions that you now recognize as foolish. You ignored the sign, not realizing the significance of your action until it was too late. As your heart pounds and races, the boulder momentarily appears to be moving in slow motion. You think about what you could do to change the outcome of your actions. *I could run ahead of the boulder and try to stop it!* Before you can even finish this thought, you realize how impossible it would be, and how foolish it sounds. You then think to yourself, *I could outrun the boulder to warn everyone in the village below about the devastation that is fast approaching!* You inevitably realize that nothing can be done to stop the boulder from rolling until it comes to a place of rest. The village in the valley is now destined to experience and suffer the consequences of your decision to push the boulder. You watch in agony, guilt, and shame, as you see the devastation and destruction left behind by your actions."

This is a simple story with a simple message. We must accept the responsibility and the consequences that come with making poor choices. We should learn from our mistakes and recognize when our actions or behavior injure others, ready to be accountable and to make amends for the harm caused to others. Oh, and it may not hurt to heed the warning signs around us. This may be a simple story, but how many of us have ignored obvious warning signs, choosing destructive behavior and actions that have devastated the lives of others, including our own?

My father made a choice to abandon his family and divorce my mother, leaving in his wake a family that was fractured, displaced, and devastated by the rolling stone that bowled us over. Poppa was truly a rolling stone! To this day, I would not be able to identify my father if he stood right in front of me. His actions and his absence, however, left an impression that our family felt for years after his departure.

In the same way, Adam made a choice to disobey God, and the effects of his action have been felt for centuries down through the generations until today. Like Adam's choice, my father's actions became a curse that affected my mother and his children. Thank God for Jesus Christ! We do not have to languish forever and live our lives under the curse of Adam and the sins of our fathers. God's purpose for salvation was to destroy the curse of Adam and Eve's disobedience and to restore our lives from the devastation and destruction caused by the effects of sin that bowl us over like a rolling stone.

Jesus Christ is God's divine act of love to redeem man's fallen nature and to save his soul from death and destruction. This redemption restores man to a right relationship that allows him to enjoy fellowship with God. After Adam committed the sin of eating the fruit from the tree, God began to demonstrate His love, concern, compassion, and justice for man's fallen state.

> Then the eyes of both of them were opened, and they realized they were naked; so they sewed fig leaves together and made coverings for themselves. Then the man and his wife heard the sound of the Lord God as he was walking in the garden in the cool of the day, and they hid from the Lord God among the trees of the garden. But the Lord

God called to the man, "Where are you?" He answered,
"I heard you in the garden, and I was afraid because I was
naked; so I hid." And he said, "Who told you that you were
naked? Have you eaten from the tree that I commanded
you not to eat from?" The Lord God made garments of
skin for Adam and his wife and clothed them. (Genesis
3:7–11, 21 NIV)

Do you see how God responded to Adam and Eve? Notice
how He came to them in the garden after Adam expressed his
fears to God and acknowledged his attempt to try to hide from
God because of his nakedness. Do you see that God did not condemn them for what they had done? Did you notice that God did
not chastise them for the obvious wrong they had committed?
Instead, God responded with mercy, kindness, and grace. God
made garments of skin, and He himself clothed them. God initiated an act of redemption by providing them with a covering
to cover their nakedness, their shame, and their guilt. God provided Adam and Eve comfort, reassurance of His love, and care
for them. He dealt with their immediate need, even though they
had committed a sin. Although there were immediate and eternal
consequences for their actions (Genesis 3:16–19), God provided
an immediate and eternal solution to overcome Satan's destructive influence and power.

"For the wages of sin is death, but the gift of God is eternal
life in Christ Jesus our Lord" (Romans 6:23 NIV).

The *plan* of salvation is God's promise to redeem the fallen
nature of man. God's *purpose* in salvation is to restore man to
God's original likeness and image. He does this through the
power of His love, His Son, and His Spirit at work in the hearts
and minds of everyone who sincerely believes in what Christ
accomplished on the cross.

"Then God said, 'Let us make man in our image, in our likeness.' So God created man in His own image, in the image of
God he created him; male and female he created them" (Genesis

1:26a–27 NIV). Every man in existence is created in the likeness of the Creator of heaven and earth. Every man has a spirit and a soul, which is housed in his physical body.

"The Lord God formed the man of the dust of the ground, and breathed into his nostrils the breath of life; and man became a living soul" (Genesis 2:7 KJV). "The Spirit of God has made me; the breath of the Almighty gives me life" (Job 33:4 NIV).

God is a Spirit, and He has a soul as well. "My *soul* is overwhelmed with sorrow to the point of death" (Matthew 26:38a, emphasis added). "Now the just shall live by faith: but if any man draw back, my *soul* shall have no pleasure in him" (Hebrews 10:38 NIV, emphasis added).

The soul of God and man is made up of the mind (intellect), the heart (emotions), and the will (ability to choose). Collectively, these make up our human nature. With the freedom she had been given, Eve was influenced by Satan and chose to disobey God. At first, Adam chose to obey God by ignoring the tree, but he was later influenced and chose to disobey God by taking the fruit from Eve. Since Eve came from Adam, and every man has come from them, we are all born with the capacity to choose the opposite of what God desires for us. Sin distorts the image and likeness of God in man. This is what is referred to as the *sinful nature*. What we call *human nature*, the ability and freedom to choose, is also condemned and regarded as the *sinful nature*. When man's choices are in rebellion against God's intentions for man, or they contradict His word, God regards these choices as sinful.

"The Lord saw how great man's wickedness on the earth had become, and that every inclination of the thoughts of his heart was only evil all the time" (Genesis 6:5 NIV).

"The heart is deceitful above all things, and desperately wicked: who can know it?" (Jeremiah 17:9 NIV).

"The acts of the sinful nature are obvious: sexual immorality, impurity and debauchery; idolatry and witchcraft; hatred, discord, jealousy, fits of rage, selfish ambition, dissensions, factions and envy; drunkenness, orgies, and the like. I warn you, as I did before, that those who live like this will not inherit the kingdom of God" (Galatians 5:19–21).

It was never God's intention for man to choose the opposite of what He desired for man. Rather, he desires that men choose Him over the influence of evil and Satan. We can only be tempted and influenced by the devil through the desires that are within us, so when we are tempted, God wants us to turn to Him instead of giving in to our temptation. God knew beforehand that man's fallen nature would make it impossible for us to follow through with the choice to live for Him. This is why He provided Jesus Christ. Even in the beginning, in the garden, God saw our need for His divine help and provided us with an eternal solution for an eternal problem. Since the beginning of time, it has been God's plan and desire to restore man to His own image and likeness.

By the power of God, Jesus Christ died and rose again so that we may experience God's love in redemption. Through faith in Jesus Christ, God's Spirit takes residence and lives within us to restore our souls and transform us back into the original image and likeness of our Creator. God's word is the source of power that provides the knowledge and inspiration that moves us to respond to God and allows Him to work in and through us to accomplish this great work.

"If you love me, you will obey what I command. And I will ask the Father, and he will give you another Counselor to be with you forever—the Spirit of truth. The world cannot accept him, because it neither sees him nor knows him. But you know him, for he lives with you and will be in you. Jesus replied, "If anyone loves me, he will obey my teaching. My Father will love him, and we will come to him and make our home with him" (John 14:15–17, 23 NIV).

Jesus explained to His disciples that men who choose to follow God's written Word express love for God through their obedience to His word. Jesus told the disciples in this passage that God's Spirit, the Counselor and the Spirit of truth, would take up residence in us, to be with us and help us. In verse 23, Christ made it clear that anyone who accepts the truth of Jesus Christ will experience a personal, intimate encounter with God.

Imagine, for a moment, that you have invited people over to enjoy good conversation and a good meal. When they arrive, you invite them in, and no sooner have you sat down to talk, but they begin to tell you how your home could be better with a few changes and a little work. At first you are startled, and soon you take offense. Not only are they criticizing your taste in decorating, but they also have the audacity to tell you the plans *they* have for your home when those changes are made. At no time have they considered your opinion, nor have they noticed a change in your attitude as they've shared all their grand ideas and plans for your home.

This is the fear many people have about the God of the Bible and the prospect of committing to faith in Jesus Christ. The fear is that God will impose His views or lifestyle on them and that they will have to give up having fun or enjoying life. Some may argue, "I am comfortable with my life the way it is, and I like the way I live. Sure, I could make some changes and do better here or there, but why should I have to change? At least I am not as bad as some other people."

Others may claim, "Have you seen how some Christians live? I hear them talking and preaching to others, but their lives are no better than anybody else's. They're getting divorced and having extramarital sex just as much as everybody else. And please don't get me started on the church and preachers who steal the money they beg for every Sunday. I'm a good person. I pay my taxes, donate to charities, and try hard to live right. That should be enough!"

Still others may even suggest, "I don't want God—or anyone else, for that matter—preaching to me about how I need to change or live my life! This is my life, and I am going to live it the way I choose!"

God initiates an invitation for us to welcome Him into our lives. Like Adam and Eve, we make the choice to either accept or reject God's invitation. "Here I am! I stand at the door and knock. If anyone hears my voice and opens the door, I will come in and eat with him, and he with me" (Revelation 3:20 NIV).

God wants us to understand that we do have a choice and that there are consequences, as there were for Adam and Eve, when we choose the opposite of what God desires for us. According to the Bible, choosing to accept Jesus Christ means believing God. His written Word says that He loves us and wants what is best for us. By choosing Jesus Christ, we are telling God that we believe He exists, according to the Bible, and we want what He wants for us. In order for us to understand God's *motive* in inviting us to allow Him into our lives, we must have a knowledge of God that allows us to trust Him and let Him in.

God loves us and cares for us. If we believe that He is concerned about us and has plans for us—that He wants to prosper us and not harm us, to give us a hope and a future, according to Jeremiah 29:11–14—then we will invite Him into our lives by placing our faith in Jesus Christ. We will then learn to live the life He wants for us, according to His word. However, if we do not believe that God is the loving, caring God He proclaims Himself to be in His word, then we will see Him as the overbearing guest we invite into our home. We will believe that He intrudes in our lives with His imposing views and opinions about how we should live, inciting hostility, discord, and rebellion.

Imagine once again the scenario of inviting a guest into your home. This time the guest is the architect who *designed* your home. When you invite him in, you are amazed at what he tells you. The architect expresses, with passion and sincere delight, a desire to remodel and upgrade your home, which he designed. With great and explicit detail, explains his intentions and his commitment to ensure the completion of the project. You are overwhelmed by the offer.

Your guest pauses when he sees the puzzled look on your face. "I'm sure you're thinking that this all sounds great," he says, "but you're wondering how much it will cost you, right?" Your discomfort over his proposal is somewhat soothed by his understanding of your concern about the cost you will pay for this project. Before you can summon the nerve to ask about the financial burden for this kind of investment, the architect amazes you further with his claim that the project will be free of charge!

"You heard me right," says the architect. "I will pay for everything. I would like to complete the plans I have for this home." You cannot believe what you are hearing! You ask, "What's the catch? This is too good to be true!" The architect replies, "There is no catch. I will pay for everything. At no cost to you, I would like to complete the plans I have shared with you. All I ask in return is that you assist me in completing the project. Whatever you cannot do, or do not know how to do, I will teach you, so you can help me finish the project." What a proposal! What would you do? The work might be difficult and cost you in time, effort, and commitment to finish what you started, but the architect has paid for everything else.

This is God's purpose for salvation. Jesus Christ has already paid the price for God's plans to remodel and upgrade our lives through the sacrifice of His life on the cross. In explicit detail, God has explained in His word all that He is willing to do to ensure the completion of His project of redemption.

> I will give you a new heart and put a new spirit in you; I will remove from you your heart of stone and give you a heart of flesh. And I will put my Spirit in you and move you to follow my decrees and be careful to keep my laws. This is what the Sovereign Lord says: On the day I cleanse you from all your sins, I will resettle your towns, and the ruins will be rebuilt. The desolate land will be cultivated instead of lying desolate in the sight of all who pass through it. They will say, "This land that was laid waste

has become like the garden of Eden; the cities that were lying in ruins, desolate and destroyed, are now fortified and inhabited." Then the nations around you that remain will know that I the Lord have rebuilt what was destroyed and have planted what was desolate. I the Lord have spoken, and I will do it. (Ezekiel 36:26–27, 33–36)

In order for God to initiate and complete His plans and purpose for this project of redemption, we must be willing to participate in the work. We begin by accepting Christ's payment for the penalty of our sins. Please note that God told Ezekiel to tell His people that when He began to fulfill His purpose of redemption in the salvation of His people, people would refer to it as a restoration of the garden of Eden. It has been God's plan since the beginning of time to restore humankind to His own image and likeness, to the way Adam and Eve were in the garden of Eden before they chose to sin against God.

Salvation is God's divine plan, His divine promise, and His divine truth. God's word is the recorded account of His love and proclamation to save, deliver, and restore humankind, through Christ, to the original image and likeness of Himself.

"This is good, and pleases God our Savior, who wants all men to be saved and to come to a knowledge of the truth. For there is one God and one mediator between God and men, the man Christ Jesus, who gave himself as a ransom for all men—the testimony given in its proper time" (1 Timothy 2:3–6 NIV).

Since the beginning, Satan has deceived—and desires to deceive—as many people as possible about the truth of God's promise and plan for redemption.

Jesus said to them, "If God were your Father, you would love me, for I came from God and now am here. I have not come on my own; but he sent me. Why is my language not clear to you? Because you are unable to hear what I say. You belong to your father, the devil, and you want to carry out your father's desire. He was a murderer from the beginning, not holding to the truth, for there is no truth in him. When he lies, he speaks his native language, for he is a liar and the father of lies. Yet, because I tell the truth, you do not believe me!" (John 8:42–45)

In 1990 I was out of college and not earning enough to pay back my student loans. I didn't have a car, so I walked or rode my bike everywhere. Fortunately, I have a brother in California who was there for me in my time of need. My plan to write and illustrate children's books was nothing more than an idea, and I had no direction on how to proceed from where I was currently standing. I actually submitted a manuscript that was accepted, but I did not have the financial resources to help cover the cost of publication.

A friend from college told me that her mother was a teacher, and she encouraged me to apply for a substitute teacher position. On the day before my first substitute teaching assignment, I saw the movie *Kindergarten Cop* and thought, *Do I really want to do this?* By January of 1991, while I was substitute teaching, I had an administrator in one ear counseling me about attending church, and an administrator in the other ear directing me to become a full-time teacher. I actually enjoyed working as a substitute, but I did not have the necessary degree in education to be hired as a full-time teacher. I had a BFA in graphic design, with no credits toward education, and I thought I would have to return to school to obtain a degree that would allow me to teach. But God had other means and a plan I was not aware of.

I believe both administrators were divinely directed by God to speak the life and light of His love into me, to give me the direction, purpose, and guidance I would need for life.

In the fall of 1992, I was hired as an art teacher! I had a full-time job, a car, and the belief that I had everything I needed, except a mate to make this life complete. But even with the new job and car, a hollow, empty feeling gnawed away on my insides. I soon discovered that a mate was not what I was missing. Actually, I began to contemplate the need and question the purpose of going to church. In my heart and mind I concluded, "If I said I believed in God and I knew this was what He wanted, why wouldn't I go?" Of course, I didn't start going right away. I had to go out to California to see my brother and make sure this was the right answer. But the answer never changed. I realize now that God was drawing me to Jesus.

In the spring of 1993, my friend "Sunshine" shared her faith with me and invited me to visit Reid Temple AME Church. The mate I desired never materialized—not for a lack of effort, mind you—but some things just don't come together when we want them or when we think they should. After my initial visit to Reid with my friend, I started attending on my own, and eventually I gave my life to Jesus Christ! I had the experience I have heard others testify to, when they felt the preacher was looking right at them, talking right to them. I definitely felt that this pastor was talking directly to me! From then on, I felt that I needed to be in church. Previously, when the school administrator had counseled me to go to church, I had explained my plan to find a mate, get married, and have some kids. *Then* I could see the need for church.

The name of Jesus Christ was not unfamiliar to me, because I remembered my oldest brother praying with my mother when she was sick. I can't remember if he and I ever had a direct conversation about Christ, but looking back, I can say that his life communicated his belief. For some reason, I recall rejecting Christ, if not being exposed to Him, through some encounter with my brother. I sensed that maybe I should know this Jesus I'd heard him talking about, but it never went any further than that. I remember drawing a picture of Jesus Christ when I attended Sunday school at my family's church in Washington, DC, but that was before we moved away in 1977. My mother attempted to take me to church when I was a teenager, but I was not interested. I had friends. Who needed church?

After I took a step of faith and walked to the front of the church to accept the invitation for salvation, a church official asked me if I knew who Christ was. I said yes. She asked if I knew that believing in Him afforded me the privilege of eternal life. After hesitating, I said no. All those previous years, I had been in the dark, not understanding the life God desired for me to have in the name of His Son. I had been without purpose, lacking guidance and direction, and when Christ had initially been offered to me, I had rejected Him.

I look back with amazement at how God sent His message of love, concern, and compassion to me through the friends and administrators that He placed on my path to give me direction. God never gave up on me. Instead, He continued to pursue me. He provided the path and gave me the sense of direction and purpose I would need to allow Him to fulfill the purposes and plans He has for me. But I had to make the choice, and I am so thankful that I did.

Believe and receive God's love offering of eternal life!

CHAPTER 5

LIVING IN THIS EXISTENCE: GOD'S FULFILLMENT THROUGH SALVATION

Jesus answered, "I am the way and the truth and the life. No one comes to the Father except through me.

—John 14:6 (NIV)

He then began to teach them that the Son of Man must suffer many things and be rejected by the elders, chief priests and teachers of the law, and that he must be killed and after three days rise again.

—Mark 8:31 (NIV)

Along this journey I have invited you to take with me, we have discovered some of what the Bible teaches about salvation, learning some of God's plan and His purpose for salvation. Within the pages of this chapter about God's fulfillment through salvation, I hope that the eyes of your heart will be enlightened and that you will experience the fulfillment and enrichment from His word that I've experienced.

At times I have asked people to imagine God coming to them personally and telling them that He desires to bless them and graciously give to them what their hearts desire. It's an intriguing idea that makes us think more about what we pray for, hope for, and live for. Based on where you are right now in your life, what would you ask of God, if you knew He would freely give it to you? What would your heart and mind ask for that would bring to you the greatest sense of fulfillment and joy out of life?

Believe it or not, there was a person who experienced this very scenario. His name was Solomon.

> At Gibeon the Lord appeared to Solomon during the night in a dream, and God said, "Ask for whatever you want me to give you." Solomon answered, "You have shown great kindness to your servant, my father David, because he was faithful to you and righteous and upright in heart. Now, O Lord my God, you have made your servant king in place of my father David. But I am only a little child and do not know how to carry out my duties. Your servant is here among the people you have chosen, a great people, too numerous to count or number. So give your servant a discerning heart to govern your people and to distinguish between right and wrong. For who is able to govern this great people of yours?" The Lord was pleased that Solomon had asked for this. So God said to him, "Since you have asked for this and not for long life or wealth for yourself, nor have asked for death of your enemies but for discernment in administering justice, I will do what you have asked. Moreover, I will give you what you have not asked for—both riches and honor—so that in your lifetime you will have no equal among kings. And if you walk in my ways and obey my statutes and commands as David your father did, I will give you a long life." (1 Kings 3:5–12a, 13–14)

Wow! I am always fascinated with this exchange between God and Solomon, and I want to use it as the backdrop for sharing some insight I've gained in understanding my own faith walk with God. It is significant in my understanding of God's plan of fulfillment through salvation.

Fulfillment is defined as "the state or quality of being fulfilled, or the completion or realization of a dream, idea or task." As I ponder the reality of this thought, I am immediately reminded of the dream of Rev. Dr. Martin Luther King Jr. Next to the life of my Lord and Savior Jesus Christ, the life of Dr. King reminds me of the influential power of hope, commitment, determination, sacrifice, and faith, when it is lived out among us for all to see. These two men dedicated their lives to serving humanity, and they spent their years in exchange for the liberation and freedom of others.

They lived with passion, giving hope to the downtrodden and spreading a message of love that lifted up the hearts and heads of the weary and the weak. They toiled and labored, suffered and persevered across many miles of prejudice, hatred, discord, jealousy, and spiritual wickedness in high places. They endured their assignments of suffering, and even in death, their lives continue to influence and affect the lives of many today. In no way am I suggesting that Dr. King should receive the same reverence due Jesus Christ, but their lives are similar in the context of explaining this matter of fulfillment.

In spite of the violence, hatred, animosity, resistance, and rejection of their own people, and the turmoil, unbelief, doubt, and criticism of others, the lives of both Jesus Christ and Dr. King prove that in living there is something worth dying for. Their fulfillment came in sacrificing their lives that others might benefit from the purpose for which they struggled and died: the freedom and liberty of humankind.

What is your heart's desire in experiencing a fulfilling life? When you close your eyes and begin to dream, where do your thoughts take you? What do you see in your mind's eye that moves you to live in this existence and stimulates you with an energy that keeps you from giving up, giving in, or losing hope? I've always believed that hope is the motivation for living. I believe that without hope we stop living, and when we stop living, we are already dead. Deep within you there is a hope, a passion, something that moves you to live. I believe that this is where your fulfillment lies.

"To this end I labor, struggling with all his energy, which so powerfully works in me" (Colossians 1:29 NIV).

God's plan for fulfillment *through salvation* is the continual manifestation of His love, expressed from one life to another. That expression is inspired or motivated by our believing in and accepting Jesus Christ as God's Son and acknowledging His death on the cross as payment for the penalty of our sins.

> Dear friends, let us love one another, for love comes from God. Everyone who loves has been born of God and knows God. Whoever does not love does not know God, because God is love. This is how God showed his love among us: He sent his one and only Son into the world that we might live through him. This is love: not that we loved God, but that he loved us and sent his Son as an atoning sacrifice for our sins. Dear friends, since God so loved us, we also ought to love one another. We love because he first loved us. If anyone says, "I love God," yet hates his brother, he is a liar. For anyone who does not love his brother, whom he has seen, cannot love God, whom he has not seen. And he has given us this command: Whoever loves God must also love his brother. (1 John 4:7–11, 19–21 NIV)

In the beginning, God created us in His image and His likeness, and then sin distorted that image, causing us to act out of the character that God intended for us in the beginning. Christ came to restore us to the image of God so that we would love Him and others the way He loves us. The fulfillment of salvation undoes the damage caused by sin in our lives, through an ongoing, intimate, and personal encounter with God. Through this encounter, by faith in Jesus Christ, we can allow God, through the life of Christ, to live in and through us so that we share the love He gives freely to us.

This is one reason why I believe that God was pleased with Solomon's request in 1 Kings 3:9 (NIV): "So give your servant a discerning heart to govern your people and to distinguish between right and wrong. For who is able to govern this great people of yours?"

By saying that he was only a little child, Solomon demonstrated humility. He did not know how to govern God's people, and he acknowledged that this was a great task for anyone to accomplish on his own. By admitting this, He was seeking God's help. I also believe that seeking wisdom from God to govern His people showed Solomon's love for God and His people, because he desired to lead them in accordance with the manner in which God would have it done. By seeking God and asking for help with his responsibilities, Solomon was expressing love for God. With God's wisdom and help, Solomon could effectively show love toward God's people.

Just as Solomon expressed a need for God's help and recognized Him as the source or provision for his need, salvation expresses to God that we are not able or sufficient in ourselves to live life in the manner He has intended us to live. By receiving salvation, we are saying to God that He is the source of life, that we need His help to live. We are like children in His sight, and we see life as a great responsibility. No, we are not all kings or rulers over multitudes of people, but we are parents, teachers, ministers, coworkers, and supervisors. We come into contact with people daily, and in our lives we are responsible for the things (homes, cars, jobs, money, etc.) that we have currently been blessed to receive from God. God desires that we, like Solomon, seek His help and guidance in living a fulfilling life, and He desires that we understand that the fulfillment of life begins with our knowing Jesus Christ.

One day I pondered deeply the meaning of a statement made by Jesus to His disciples in the gospel of John. "The thief comes only to steal and kill and destroy; I have come that they may have life, and have it to the full" (John 10:10 NIV).

"I have come that they may have *life*." I thought about that sincerely. He came so that I may have *life*. And then I thought, *Lord, if you came that I may have* life, *then what was it I had before you came?* He seemed to answer, "You just existed before. You weren't living as I intended for you to live, because the life I intended for you to live can't be lived without me or apart from me. The life I came for you to live, I desire for you to live to the fullest and forever."

"Jesus said to her, 'I am the resurrection and the life. He who believes in me will live, even though he dies; and whoever lives and believes in me will never die. Do you believe this?'" (John 11:25–26 NIV).

I thought about it. I just existed. It was like being alive, but in a coma at the same time. God has a life planned for us that He invites us to enjoy and live with Him not apart from Him. It is a life that is both spiritual and eternal and because of sin we can neither live spiritually or eternally without God.

"So I say live by the Spirit, and you will not gratify the desires of the sinful nature. For the sinful nature desires what is contrary to the Spirit, and the Spirit what is contrary to the sinful nature. They are in conflict with each other, so that you do not do what you want. Those who belong to Christ Jesus have crucified the sinful nature with its passions and desires. Since we live by the Spirit, let us keep in step with the Spirit" (Galatians 5:16–17, 24–25 NIV).

He created us to experience a life that includes His presence, His power, and His person—not just around us, but also in us and through us. God desires that we know Him as intimately as He knows us.

"In him was life, and that life was the light of men. The true light that gives light to every man was coming into the world. Yet to all who received him, to those who believed in his name, he gave the right to become children of God" (John 1: 4, 9, 12 NIV).

"Since, then, you have been raised with Christ, set your hearts on things above, where Christ is seated at the right hand of God. Set your minds on things above, not on earthly things. For you died, and your life is now hidden with Christ in God. When Christ, who is your life, appears, then you also will appear with him in glory" (Colossians 3:1–3 NIV).

God's fulfillment in salvation is accomplished in me by my allowing the person of Jesus Christ to live in and through me. This begins when I believe in Jesus Christ as the Son of God and accept His sacrifice of life and shed blood on the cross as payment for the penalty of my sins. The life God desires for me to live is hidden with Christ in God. God wants me to seek Him to find the life He desires for me to live, and He promises that if I do, it will be both fulfilling and rewarding!

This is the life that Jesus came to give us. He came and died for us so that He might live through us and allow the life He lived in the Bible to be expressed through us. The life He came for us to live to the fullest is a life of compassion, love, peace, mercy, kindness, gentleness, joy, faithfulness, and self-control. It is a life that demonstrates what God is able to do with someone who is willing to live by faith in Him, someone who is willing to trust His word by believing in Him to fulfill the promises, plans, and purposes He proclaims in the scriptures.

I have a friend named Jeff, whom I love as a brother, and who is also my brother in Christ. I have had the privilege of watching God intimately unfold His plans and purposes in this man's life. Jeff told me that, before coming to Christ, he remembered watching a well-known preacher from the Baltimore–Washington metropolitan area on television. Deep within, for the first time in his life, Jeff felt the hope of his calling and fulfillment. While the preacher was speaking, Jeff said to himself that he liked what the preacher was doing and believed he could do it too. Jeff was stirred in his soul and immediately began to seek a place where he could hear more of those inspiring messages, which he now desired to deliver himself. This inspiration led him to Reid Temple AME Church, where he began to hear the soul-stirring proclamations of Rev. Dr. Lee P. Washington. Not long after hearing the voice of God through these jars of clay, Jeff believed in Jesus Christ as the Son of God and committed his life to one day becoming a minister of the gospel of Jesus Christ.

Jeff saw his own fulfillment by watching two ministers preach the gospel of Jesus Christ. God used these men to share a life-giving, life-changing message of life and hope to Jeff—one that he could not resist. When I met Jeff at Reid Temple some time later, the word around Reid Temple was that Jeff was a walking Bible. If you wanted to hear a word from God, you needed to talk with Jeff. I must admit I too was amazed at his breadth of knowledge of the Bible and his ability to share it with passion, clarity, and authority. I was impressed, as everyone else was, but soon, without my knowing it, God initiated a plan for me to get to know Jeff, the man—not just Jeff, the minister.

One fateful day, I was privileged to be in Jeff's company at his home, talking and fellowshipping with him. No doubt, being in the company of one who was regarded as a walking Bible was enough to make one's head swell, but I could really sense that God wanted me to listen to the man and not the minister. That day changed my life. I soon began to hear the voice of a man broken by life's troubles, afflicted in his soul, and in pain. I could hear the soft, gentle voice of wisdom saying to me, "Listen to him." Since then, I have felt that God wanted me to listen to Jeff as a man and not a walking Bible, for his soul, though he is a Christian, has troubles, and he needs someone to talk to.

Jeff and I spent many hours and days talking with one another. Most times, he talked and I listened. At a moment's notice, Jeff could pour out his wealth of knowledge from studying the scripture, and the ministry of the Word of God would just kick in.

But he was also pouring out his heart and soul and the pain of his search for fulfillment. Without realizing it at the time, I was hearing the reality of the divine and the human, trying to find rest and peace and coexistence within this one man.

Without warning, our lives took different turns, and Jeff and I spent less and less time sharing together. Before I knew it, we rarely saw each other. One time when we did talk, I reminded him that God told Moses to lead the Israelites from Egypt to the Promised Land. I told Jeff that I believed there was a promised place for us after salvation—in this life as well as in the life to come. I said I believed that before we left this earth, God had a place of fulfillment that would be our testimony to others about God's fulfillment through salvation.

Jeff eventually left Reid Temple to accept a position as assistant pastor at Zion Church under the pastoral leadership of Rev. Keith Battle. I learned that sometime during his journey to become a preacher, my friend Jeff had failed at a suicide attempt. Although he had become a minister of the gospel—which I believe was divinely inspired by God to get Jeff to hope and life—God also wanted to allow Jeff to experience more of His Son living in and through him. Jeff had been troubled from his childhood by low self-esteem and the pressures of being a husband and father, a provider and protector for his family. The reality of his troubles, which Jesus said we would have in this life, caused Jeff to seriously consider taking his own life. Jeff was losing the battle of life, a life in which God promised we would experience victory through faith in Jesus Christ. Jeff was harassed in his soul about his inability to provide for his family, which produced in him a great source of anger and frustration. No doubt, that further lowered his self-esteem and made the little child within him feel worse.

After his attempt to take his own life, Jeff received counseling, and it was there that he discovered his personal demon of low self-esteem from childhood. Today, at the time of writing this book, Jeff earns enough money to pay for all of his household needs. He provides marriage counseling at Zion Church, helping other couples, with the help of scripture and faith, to overcome the same kinds of trouble he experienced in his own marriage. Was Jeff's life purpose fulfilled by becoming a minister of the gospel and assistant pastor, or was it in the continual growth and development of his person through his saving faith in Jesus Christ? Could it have been both?

To *fulfill* means "to carry out, or to bring to realization, as a prophecy or promise. To bring to an end, to finish or complete, as a period of time, or to satisfy requirements or obligations." Three of the last seven words spoken by Jesus on the cross were, "It is finished" (John 19:30b NIV). Down through the ages after the garden of Eden, God promised and proclaimed, through His prophets in the Old Testament, that the fulfillment of His plan and purpose was the restoration of humankind to His image and His likeness. When Christ said, "It is finished," he was proclaiming that what God had spoken in the beginning and had proclaimed over the centuries was now done through His sacrifice of life and death on the cross.

God was bringing to an end Satan's ability to hold humankind hostage, enslaved by the penalty of their sins. Christ's death on the cross satisfied God's need for atonement and allowed humankind to experience and enjoy with Him what He had desired since Adam and Eve's sin in the garden. Humankind now had the opportunity to experience liberation from sin and to be restored to the original image and likeness of the Creator. All we have to do is believe in what Jesus did on the cross, and God will spend the rest of our lifetimes allowing us to experience the process of being restored to His likeness and His image, living life to the fullest in this existence.

What does fulfillment look like in the face of adversity or in a life decimated by disaster and calamity? How can one hope for fulfillment when all they have known is disappointment, discouragement, and doubt? Surrounded and overwhelmed with debt, sin, frustration, and the feeling that we will never get beyond where we are currently, how is it possible to entertain the idea of fulfillment? In a world of darkness where there is so much death, hatred, hostility, abuse, neglect, violence, and increasing negativity, is fulfillment even a possibility? If you have contemplated suicide, do you believe that fulfillment is a possibility for you?

I remember sharing my faith with a former student, now an adult mother of four children. I suggested that possibly life itself was a gift of fulfillment for her, since she had contemplated and attempted suicide during her childhood. Had she succeeded in committing suicide, she would not have experienced the joy of motherhood, we would never have met, and I would not have had the privileged opportunity of leading her to rededicate her life to Christ.

Years before my own life began to unravel and spiral out of control as an adult Christian, I had been told to find something to reflect upon that inspired or motivated me. This turned out to be some of the most influential, wise advice I received during my adult life. As I journeyed through the misfortune of a failed marriage, experiencing separation and divorce, God challenged me to look inward and take inventory of my soul. Through my encounter with the darkness of my own soul—dealing with my own pride, rebellion, shame, guilt, hurt, anger, and frustration—I saw God display His power, demonstrate His love, and distribute His grace toward me. He manifested Himself in ways that reminded me that He loved me and that His plans for me did not include failure, defeat, or living in cynicism, doubt, grief, or unbelief.

I remember when a friend asked me how I was dealing with the anger of a failed marriage and the consequences that come with divorce. I told my friend that I had to see myself in a better place, and every day I made it my mission to make progress toward that place. While traveling to and from work and on the weekends, I listened to sermons and speeches by the Rev. Dr. Martin Luther King Jr., and I shared what I was learning with others.

During this journey toward that "better place," I discovered journaling, and I wrestled with my inner man to get reconnected to God and remain close to Him, determined not to let go until God blessed me. I watched movies like *Men of Honor*, *Glory Road*, *Glory*, *The Patriot*, *Kingdom of Heaven*, *A Time to Kill*, *Man on Fire*, *John Q*, and *The Hurricane and Ali*. These stories motivated me and inspired within me the spiritual fortitude and internal resolve I would need to experience the fulfillment I was seeking and not succumb to whatever sought to keep me down, defeated, or discouraged.

I learned about the strategy of *positive self-talk*: things we can say to ourselves to redirect us when our minds, circumstances, or both begin to make us feel unsettled, anxious, or upset. I said to myself, "I am not a victim in my circumstances" and "I am not above injustice." This kept me from adopting a "woe is me" or "why me?" mentality that would ensnare me in a hopeless attitude of despair and misery. Though I struggled with maintaining a consistent, vibrant prayer life, God continued to supply of His Spirit and provide timely words of encouragement, comfort, and inspiration.

As I wrote in my journal and spent devotional time in His word, He kept me going and gave me courage and confidence to stand firm in the face of misfortune, loss, and grief. Two such passages came from David himself.

"You, O Lord, keep my lamp burning; my God turns my darkness into light. With your help I can advance against a troop; with my God I can scale a wall" (Psalm 18:29 NIV).

"Though an army besiege me, my heart will not fear; though war break out against me, even then I will be confident" (Psalm 27:3 NIV).

During my greatest moments of weakness—feeling weary and worn from the weight of financial debt, depression, and the gnawing sense of discontentment and dissatisfaction of being in a season of life that was difficult to handle on my own—I saw the greatness of God's unfailing love. He aided and supported me in my time of need in ways I had never known of or encountered before. As trying and challenging as this season has been, it has also been rewarding and uplifting to see the arm of the Lord revealed to me in a way that reminded me of His care and concern for me as His child. I watched Him display His power, demonstrate His love, and distribute His grace in situations and circumstances that made me feel that things would only get worse. He helped me to grow in the confidence that He is with me to help me and bless me. He challenged me to believe and not resign myself to doubt—and to wait with expectancy for His glory to be revealed!

"We do not want you to be uninformed, brothers, about the hardships we suffered in the province of Asia. We were under great pressure, far beyond our ability to endure, so that we despaired even of life. Indeed, in our hearts we felt the sentence of death. But this happened that we might not rely on ourselves but on God, who raises the dead. He has delivered us from such a deadly peril, and he will deliver us. On him we have set our hope that he will continue to deliver us, as you help us by your prayers" (2 Corinthians 1:8–11a NIV).

In this context, I discovered the peace that passes all understanding and began to trust God more, despite what my circumstances were saying to me. I also began to see and hear more clearly the internal noise within me that came from within my own soul, discouraging my faith and emphasizing emotion over trusting God and His promises. God's faithfulness in response to my misfortune pushed me to push myself to trust and believe Him more and to acknowledge the grace and mercy He performed daily. His intervention contradicted the circumstances that sought to make me believe that I would not make it.

I saw God's blessing of others as a reminder to me that He would do the same for me, if I believed and trusted Him through my troubles, for He is not a respecter of persons, and He is the same yesterday, today, and forever. Watching my oldest brother ascend to the office of Fire Chief of the Prince George's County Fire Department was a huge source of inspiration to me. It helped me to keep believing in God and trusting Him, despite my circumstances. It was an important moment for our family as well, especially when my brother asked me to speak on his behalf before the County Council prior to his being sworn in. I'd had faith that God would help my brother and bless him, and His promotion challenged me to have that same faith that God would act in my life too.

"Forget the former things; do not dwell on the past. See, I am doing a new thing! Now it springs up; do you not perceive it? I am making a way in the desert and streams in the wasteland" (Isaiah 43:18–19 NIV).

Fulfillment in salvation requires me to perceive, in the midst of trouble and misfortune, the divine power of God at work in, through, and around me that helps me walk in the midst of trouble. Recognizing and acknowledging Him drives me to trust in God's kindness and mercy to preserve my life. I can still be positive and productive in my knowledge of Christ, believing that I will prosper, even when my current circumstances reflect depletion and disappointment.

I challenged myself to become deliberate in developing the *spiritual eyesight* required to see God at work doing the "new things" He declared in His word. I gave thanks daily for the evidence of His loving presence that kept me positive and assured me that He was with me, no matter how dark the moment or difficult the day. I began to speak to specific people—people who were headed where I was trying to get to, or who had been down the path I was traveling. That inspired me to forget what was behind me and to press forward, push through, and persevere beyond what the past was trying to keep before me.

My mother, sister, and I met regularly for Bible study, once a month for over six years, and we witnessed the power of God's word and His Spirit enlightening us and empowering us to walk with His light toward victory! Our Bible study theme was "Believing God for a Better Quality of Life." The woman with the issue of blood (Matthew 9; Mark 5; Luke 8) and Peter's encounter with Christ when he walked on water (Matthew 14:27–33) became inspirational figures for me to reflect upon during my journey toward the better place. For a brief period of time, even Mother Teresa became a figure of inspiration to help me navigate through the challenges, obstacles, and opportunities that lay ahead of me.

I continued to go to church, and even when my circumstances made it difficult for me to go consistently, I was determined to redevelop a close, intimate faith walk with God again. Whatever I heard in my private time that inspired me, I found ways to share with others, which reinforced what He had said to me and gave hope to others. From 2003 through 2011, I wrote in my journal, which helped me to identify more quickly my feelings and the reasons for them. I identified words or word pictures, i.e., feeling sad like a wilted flower, that helped me articulate those feelings.

Finally, five years after my intentional decision to go through the grieving process after my divorce, God allowed me to experience a breakthrough during the summer of 2011. I was led to start a devotional message ministry, *His Intimate Imminence*, which I distributed to the 203 units of my apartment complex. The inspiration to start the devotional message ministry, to share my faith with the tenants of my apartment complex, was inspired by the overwhelming sense of confidence that God was intimately present with me, no matter what I was facing. I had come to know God, who proclaims Himself as *Immanuel*, "God with us." Before long, my season of greatest trial as an adult Christian also became an extraordinary season of renewal, revival, and spiritual resurrection!

"'Because he loves me,' says the Lord, 'I will rescue him; I will protect him, for he acknowledges my name. He will call upon me, and I will answer him; I will be with him in trouble, I will deliver him and honor him. With long life will I satisfy him and show him my salvation'" (Psalm 91:14–16 NIV).

I believe that the true fulfillment of salvation in Jesus Christ is the continual, consistent experience of an intimate, personal encounter with God throughout our lives. This consistent, continual experience with God causes us to grow in the assurance that God is with us to help us and be with us, that we may see Him and experience the fulfillment of His word at work in our lives.

According to Psalm 91:16, God wants to *show His salvation* to the person who loves Him. So I see salvation as something more than a momentary decision when I make a confession for Christ in order to secure a reservation in heaven. Salvation becomes an ongoing encounter, where I am engaged in an interactive relationship with God, through faith in Jesus Christ, that allows me to see God at work in my life.

According to Psalm 91:14–16, God wants to *rescue and protect the person who acknowledges His name.* God wants to answer those who call out to Him. He wants to be with them in trouble, deliver them, honor them, and satisfy them. Some people may have wealth and material goods beyond what they can ever spend and enjoy in one lifetime, but how many can say that they are satisfied by an awareness of and access to the wealth of God's intimate love?

Some people know the fulfillment that comes from personal ambition, determination, and worldly achievement, but have they encountered or given honor to the one who is able to change things that are not as they ought to be and to make all things beautiful in their time? Have they encountered the one whose grace extends beyond their limitations to do exceeding abundantly above anything they could ask, think, or imagine? Is life truly about "pulling ourselves up by our own bootstraps," or is God the author and finisher of each man's fulfillment? To the person who has known only abuse, suffering, hardship, calamity, and misfortune, could *relief* be a measure of fulfillment? What about the many men and women who surrender their lives in service to their country and return from combat torn, tattered, and sometimes physically, mentally, or emotionally shattered? What does fulfillment look like for them?

What about the person who strives, perseveres, endures, struggles, and continues to press forward—but no matter how much progress he appears to make, it seems like his destination and goals for fulfillment drift further away or never seem to materialize? Is the goal and destination alone the measure of their fulfillment?

Let's consider an illustration from David's life, revealed in scripture during a season in his life when he was between the proclaimed promise and the fulfillment of that promise that he would become king. Decide for yourself whether he encountered any measure of fulfillment. This may provide insight and a source of encouragement for you in your journey toward the fulfillment God intends for you through faith in Jesus Christ.

In 1 Samuel 16, we are introduced to David as a young man, the youngest of the seven sons of Jesse. God had determined that David would be the next king of Israel. David was anointed to be king, but Israel already had a king: Saul. Some time later, King Saul requested that David serve him and become a leader in his army. By 1 Samuel 17, David had defeated Goliath and was being celebrated for his bravery and actions in serving under Saul's authority and defending God's glory against the enemies of God's people.

Jealousy, fear, and envy began to shroud Saul's heart, and he became enraged by David's celebrity status among the people and the possibility that David might take his throne. He plotted to kill David. In 1 Samuel 18–22, David's prominence as a leader and his success in battle caused him to grow in stature in the eyes of the people. Saul's jealousy and intent to kill David grew as well. Saul attacked David but failed in his attempt to kill him. Then David was on the run from Saul, not understanding why the king was seeking his life.

By 1 Samuel 22, David was seeking refuge in a cave. This was not exactly the place one would expect to find a celebrated, successful man—faithful in his service to God and responsibility for others—who had been anointed to become king. Even in the face of hostility and the threat of death, David did not seek vengeance or try to retaliate against the one who sought to take his life. For the moment, it appeared that the anointing and promise of David's ascension to the throne was about to be extinguished before it materialized. A man after God's own heart, he was currently in a situation that appeared to threaten God's promise to him that he would experience a measure of fulfillment, blessing, and prosperity.

Life's troubles and momentary circumstances have a way of challenging our faith, causing us to doubt that He will fulfill what He has promised and perform what He has spoken. According to God's word, faith teaches us that He will make use of misfortune, calamity, and troubles in the process of bringing us to places of abundance, prosperity, and fulfillment.

After his anointing and a season of success and celebration, David found himself in a cave, trying to stay alive and trying to understand how his life had unraveled so quickly and brought him to his current situation. The man who had defeated Goliath by faith, who had experienced one military victory after another, who had been anointed for kingship, was hiding in a cave, probably disillusioned about the circumstances that had brought him to that point in his life. His questions were probably like ours.

Where am I? How did I get here? Why am I here? Why is this happening to me? Will I ever get out of this place? Is this what life is about? I achieved what I thought would be fulfilling, but I still feel unfulfilled. What now? Is this what living by faith is all about? Am I where I am because of sin? Do I lack faith? If I have faith, why do things seem to be getting worse? Why do my nights seem to last longer than my days? Trusting and believing God seems to bring more hardship, misfortune, and calamity into my life than when I was living in ignorance apart from Him. Is that possible? As a believer in Christ, shouldn't I experience wealth, prosperity, and power? Should a Christian be depressed? Does God love me? Is God with me? Has He forgotten me?

Is it possible for a Christian to come to a place in his faith walk when the bottom falls out, when he seems to be looking up from the proverbial mat, wondering how he got there? Can I get back up? *Will* I get back up? Do I even *want* to get back up? Is it possible for a Christian who is living a life of purpose and fulfillment to have that life snatched away from him without warning? Must he spend a season trying to recover from what happened, trying to envision a way to move from that "cave" to a better place?

We may be on the run from abuse, violence, hatred, jealousy, envy, debt, divorce, disappointment, disillusionment, discouragement, debilitating illness, professional displacement, loss of economic stability, the past, fear of failure, mistakes, momentary setbacks, rejection, family dysfunction, and the reality of misfortune and calamity that come from the troubles of life. But eventually, we all find ourselves, like David, in a "cave," seeking asylum and refuge.

"The seed that fell among thorns stands for those who hear, but as they go on their way they are choked by life's worries, riches and pleasures, and they do not mature" (Luke 8:14 NIV).

We begin to seek asylum in pleasures, sex, money, power, alcohol, drugs, pornography, food, self-pity, doubt, worry, anxiety, depression, emotional/mental disorders, cynicism, anger, violence, withdrawal, and isolation. Asylum may come in the form of unhealthy relationships that make us dependent on people rather than God, or the illusion of what television and the world proclaim as the way to success and fulfillment.

"But they soon forgot what he had done and did not wait for his counsel. In the desert they gave in to their craving; in the wasteland they put God to the test. So he gave them what they asked for, but sent a wasting disease upon them. Then they despised the pleasant land; they did not believe his promise. They grumbled in their tents and did not obey the LORD. So he swore to them with uplifted hand that he would make them fall in the desert, make their descendants fall among the nations and scatter them throughout the lands" (Psalm 106:13–15, 24–27 NIV).

"Do not store up for yourselves treasures on earth, where moth and rust destroy, and where thieves break in and steal. But store up for yourselves treasures in heaven, where moth and rust do not destroy, and where thieves do not break in and steal. For where your treasure is, there your heart will be also. But seek first his kingdom and his righteousness, and all these things will be given to you as well" (Matthew 6:19–21, 33 NIV).

Where will I turn? To whom will I look during the "cave" season of life? During David's season in the cave, he learned that God goes everywhere His anointed one goes. He was about to discover that the same God who had anointed him to be king, given him great victories, honored him in the sight of men, and helped him escape the threat of death would also love and support him during his time in the cave. God sent people to David— his family, his father, his brothers, and people who were described as being in debt, distressed, and discontented—to rally around him and become a source of encouragement.

In my faith walk with Christ, I am discovering that God uses my cave season to express His love to me in ways that are not conventional, logical, or expected but clearly show me that He is present with me, concerned and caring.

"A father to the fatherless, a defender of widows, is God in his holy dwelling. God sets the lonely in families, he leads forth the prisoners with singing" (Psalm 68:5–6a NIV).

When God sent the prophet Samuel to David's home to anoint the king who would replace Saul, David's father, Jesse, did not think David was worthy to be present. David declared in Psalm 27 that he felt forsaken by his father, but in David's greatest time of need, Jesse was present at the cave to support his son. After being anointed king, David had brought food to his brothers in Saul's army—as the soldiers cowered in fear of Goliath and the Philistines—and David's brothers had expressed their disdain for him. But those very men who had rejected and disregarded

David were at his side in the cave, supporting him during his time of refuge there. Greater than our desire for fulfillment is experiencing the fulfillment of scripture in a way that enables us to transcend the dark and difficult times of life and empowers us to live and experience the victorious power of Christ's resurrection!

One of the greatest rewards of my life is my intimate relationship with God that allows me to see the fulfillment of scripture in my life through the lives of biblical characters such as David. God assures me that He is present with me, as He was with Moses, Joshua, David, and others in scripture, and He affirms His love for me. I have learned to declare to God in my prayers that as He was with Moses and Joshua, I know He is with me. I believe that God is saying to me the very same words He told Joshua (Joshua 1:5) to help him prepare to lead God's people from the wilderness into the Promised Land. Sometimes I pray, "Father, thank you for remembering me as you remembered Noah during the flood."

Greater than experiencing personal fulfillment, I was encountering the fulfillment of scripture and God's plans for my fulfillment—as I learned to walk with Him by faith. It was God's plan of fulfillment for Abraham to have a son, for Noah to build the ark, for Moses to lead the Israelites, for Mary to birth our Lord and Savior, Jesus Christ, and for each of us who believes to experience the fulfillment of His person, presence, power, and promises in His word.

Do we seek the fulfillment of experiencing God's person, presence, and power in our lives as Christians, even as we seek to become wealthy, powerful, and successful? It was God's plan of fulfillment for David—a child shepherd living a life of obscurity—to ascend to the throne of Israel and reign as king. What is intriguing about God's plan of fulfillment for David's life is the season of transition that David encountered—*after* being celebrated and honored while serving in Saul's army, and *before* he became king. It is intriguing to me, because we normally don't associate the fulfillment and blessing of God's promises with a season like the one David endured while he was on the run from Saul.

What if part of God's plan for fulfillment in salvation is for a Christian to endure and persevere through misfortune and calamity as Christ did? Consider the apostle Paul's declaration of the fulfillment he sought to experience (Philippians 3:10), and ask yourself how often you hear Christians seeking that same kind of fulfillment in life. How many Christians reflect on the type of fulfillment *God* seeks to accomplish in and through us—versus the type of fulfillment *we* generally seek to encounter?

Consider also that the apostle Paul was imprisoned during much of his faith walk with Christ, yet his letters make up a large portion of the New Testament and have influenced the lives of millions for over two thousand years! How often do our desires for fulfillment align with God's will? How often do we ask God to help us display Christ's character as we pray for and aspire to personal and professional success, financial gain, and material blessings? Faith in Christ requires a balanced heavenly perspective. Sometimes we will encounter the power of Christ's resurrection in the form of great victories, achievement, advancement, elevation, favor, and prosperity. And sometimes we will share in the fellowship of Christ's sufferings, which may be accompanied by misfortune, loss, injustice, and grief.

"For it has been granted to you on behalf of Christ not only to believe on him, but also to suffer for him" (Philippians 1:29 NIV).

"I want to know Christ and the power of his resurrection and the fellowship of sharing in his sufferings, becoming like him in his death, and so, somehow, to attain to the resurrection from the dead" (Philippians 3:10–11 NIV).

In reading about David's experience at the cave, I am intrigued by the descriptions of the people God sent to him and the ultimate impact that David's anointing had on them. David was on the run, taking refuge from King Saul's death threat. His life in the cave was a far cry from his previous life of being celebrated as one who had killed tens of thousands, as one who had been honored in the sight of God and men, as one who had served Saul in the palace.

But David discovered, as he declared in Psalm 27, that the Lord had not forsaken him. God sent David's family to him, along with a group of people who were described as being in debt, discontented, and in distress. David, who was himself distressed, was surrounded by a group of distressed people. Logic and conventional wisdom would declare that the people God surrounded David with would have ultimately been the undoing of his progress toward his destiny. How could these people benefit David, when from all appearances they had nothing to offer but their distress, debt, and discontentment? Conventional wisdom would advise surrounding oneself with positive-minded, progressive people who are going somewhere. How could David's companions be beneficial to him, when they appeared to be of no benefit to themselves?

Beyond their external descriptions and internal challenges, I believe that their main benefit to David was in having been sent to him by God. I believe their presence alone became a source of strength to David. Life has taught me that external circumstances do not define the ultimate value of a person's significance or the true measure of his quality. A person who suffers is no less valuable, significant, or important than one who does not—and vice versa. Scripture reveals that misfortune will test the genuine quality and integrity of a person's character. Scripture also declares that my misfortune and grief allow me to be a source of encouragement to others who encounter misfortune. The comfort I receive from God during my cave season of life positions me to share that comfort with others.

"But the Lord said to Samuel, 'Do not consider his appearance or his height, for I have rejected him. The LORD does not look at the things man looks at. Man looks at the outward appearance, but the LORD looks at the heart'" (1 Samuel 16:7 NIV).

"Praise be to the God and Father of our Lord Jesus Christ, the Father of compassion and the God of all comfort, who comforts us in all our troubles, so that we can comfort those in any trouble with the comfort we ourselves have received from God. If we are distressed, it is for your comfort and salvation, if we are comforted, it is for your comfort, which produces in you patient endurance of the same sufferings we suffer. And our hope for you is firm, because we know that just as you share in our sufferings, so also you share in our comfort" (2 Corinthians 1:3–4, 6–7 NIV).

"We were under great pressure, far beyond our ability to endure, so that we despaired even of life. Indeed, in our hearts we felt the sentence of death. But this happened that we might not rely on ourselves but on God, who raises the dead. On him we have set our hope that he will continue to deliver us, as you help us by your prayers" (2 Corinthians 1:8b–11a).

"If you falter in times of trouble, how small is your strength!" (Proverbs 24:10).

Undoubtedly, David's previous renown inspired those who now stood with him during this season of asylum in the cave. All throughout scripture, we see God move in unconventional ways, using illogical means to accomplish great and miraculous acts for those He loves. In His faithfulness, He promises to preserve, protect, and provide for them. While shepherding his father's sheep, serving Saul in the palace, fighting on the battlefield, and hiding in the cave, David discovered that God remained intimately present with him and manifested His love toward him in ways that continued to uplift, uphold, and elevate David, despite the momentary conditions of his current circumstances. Whether he faced lions and bears in protecting the sheep, fought the enemies of Israel and defeated Goliath, or evaded the wrath of a man who sought to kill him, David experienced the supernatural, miraculous power of God to equip, enable, and empower him to be victorious.

The people who came to the cave were evidence of God's compassion toward David, God's provision of support in David's time of need. I also believe that the people who were moved to come to David's aid at the cave represented two biblical principles. Psalm 20:1–2 supports my belief that the people who came to the cave demonstrated God's compassion toward David, and 2 Timothy 2:22 reveals insight on the principle of Christian fellowship, highlighted through the relationships between David and the people around him.

"May the LORD answer you when you are in distress; may the name of the God of Jacob protect you. May he send you help from the sanctuary and grant you support from Zion" (Psalm 20:1–2 NIV).

"Flee the evil desires of youth, and pursue righteousness, faith, love and peace, along with those who call on the Lord out of a pure heart" (2 Timothy 2:22 NIV).

The word *distress* is mentioned in Psalm 20:1, and I believe that the distress David felt in the cave was not born out of fear of Saul as much as it was the anxiety of running for his life, trying to escape the wrath of a man whose jealousy was out of control. David had killed a lion and a bear, defeated Goliath, and led the army of Israel to victory in battle against the enemies of Israel, so I do not believe that he feared Saul or that his distress was born out of fear. In fact, the *New International Version* of the Bible notes that Psalms 57, 59, and 142 were written specifically at a time when Saul was threatening David's life and David was seeking refuge in the cave. Verses from these psalms give us insight into David's thoughts and emotions during this season he was in the cave.

"Have mercy on me, O God, have mercy on me, for in you my soul takes refuge. I will take refuge in the shadow of your wings until the disaster has passed. They spread a net for my feet—I was bowed down in distress" (Psalm 57:1, 6a NIV).

"Deliver me from my enemies, O God; protect me from those who rise up against me. O my Strength, I watch for you; you, O God, are my fortress, my loving God" (Psalm 59:1, 9 NIV).

"I cry aloud to the LORD; I lift up my voice to the LORD for mercy. I pour out my complaint before him; before him I tell my trouble. When my spirit grows faint within me, it is you who know my way. Listen to my cry for I am in desperate need; rescue me from those who pursue me, for they are too strong for me" (Psalm 142: 1–3a, 6 NIV).

In reflecting on Psalm 20:2, I believe that the people who came to David's aid at the cave represented the help and support from Zion that God would provide to preserve and protect him and to prepare him for his destiny as king over Israel. In response to David's prayers and petitions, God sent him people from Zion who would be compassionate and comforting, a source of strength and encouragement to him, because they could identify with how David felt. Through their fellowship with David, God would bless them and make them great—despite their circumstances of being in debt, distressed, and discontent. Faith in Christ has taught me that God will make use of His power to change *me* in my circumstances—making me better, stronger, and wiser—without necessarily changing the conditions He is using to accomplish the changes in me.

The words of 2 Timothy 2:22 encourage believers to seek out those "who call on the Lord out of a pure heart." The principle of Christian fellowship was acted out in the relationship that developed between David and the people. The people experienced internal (discontent) and external (debt) challenges that created distress, but their distress was also associated with their concern, regard, or compassion for David and his circumstances. Their concern for David compelled them to go to his aid. The people who sought out David regarded him as a man after God's own heart. God's love for David was expressed through their concern for David and their willingness to act upon that concern by supporting him with their physical presence. I believe that this support became a great source of encouragement to David during this season of his life. From a heavenly perspective, I also see the fulfillment of salvation being played out in this relationship between David and the people who came to the cave to support him.

"But I have a baptism to undergo, and how distressed I am until it is completed" (Luke 12:50 NIV).

Christ is the anointed King of Kings who was sent to us: people who are in debt to sin, distressed in this world, and discontented. God, full of compassion and mercy, sent us help and support from the throne of His sanctuary. He sent help from the sanctuary of His grace in the form of His Son, Jesus Christ. The help God sent us from the sanctuary was to save us from the threat of death, the debt of sin, the wrath of Satan's jealousy over God's love for us as the apple of His eye, and the distress caused by the troubles we face in this world. Like the people who were sent to David, God compels us to seek the King of Kings, Christ, and through the anointing of His person, we are transformed by His presence. In our fellowship with Him, His power causes us to become influential in service to Him.

In Luke 12:50, we see the Lord's distress, disclosed and articulated from the soul of His humanity, as He faced the reality of His destiny, the purpose God had planned for Him—to save our souls. Likewise, David and the people who had come to him experienced God's plan of fulfillment for them, which brought along with it the distress God allowed them to experience during their cave season. I do not believe that the Lord's distress described in Luke 12:50 was a distress born out of fear. I believe it was normal anxiety derived from the external forces and internal human dilemma that pressed against Him in His desire to experience the fulfillment of God's plan for His life in being the source of salvation for all humanity. Jesus spoke of his distress—feelings of pressure without and within—that came from the reality of the burden He faced in fulfilling the calling on His life: suffering and dying for the redemption and salvation of humanity. Also, scripture teaches us that perfect loves drives out fear, so Jesus rested in the confidence that God the Father would protect Him and preserve His life. We know this to be true, for whenever Jesus discussed the crucifixion, He always concluded with the promise of being raised again!

"There is no fear in love. But perfect love drives out fear, because fear has to do with punishment. The one who fears is not made perfect in love" (1 John 4:18 NIV).

"From that time on Jesus began to explain to his disciples that he must go to Jerusalem and suffer many things at the hands of the elders, chief priests and teachers of the law, and that he must be killed and on the third day be raised to life" (Matthew 16:21 NIV).

Faith teaches us to grow in our confidence and assurance that God will hear us and help us in our troubles, preserve our lives, protect us, and provide for us in every season of life—despite the difficulty of our circumstances. We must believe this, because God is love, and perfect love, God's love, drives out fear. Resolute trust in God drives out fear from within me in the face of misfortune, injustice, and loss and replaces it with peace, joy, and hope. Faith in God challenges me to become perfect in my trust, confidence, and assurance that God will hear me and help me, no matter what!

"Shadrach, Meshach and Abednego replied to the king, 'O Nebuchadnezzar, we do not need to defend ourselves before you in this matter. If we are thrown into the blazing furnace, the God we serve is able to save us from it, and he will rescue us from your hand, O king. But even if he does not, we want you to know, O king, that we will not serve your gods or worship the image of gold you have set up" (Daniel 3:16–18 NIV).

"O LORD, God of our fathers, are you not the God who is in heaven? You rule over all the kingdoms of the nations. Power and might are in your hand and no one can withstand you. If calamity comes upon us, whether the sword of judgment, or plague or famine, we will stand in your presence before this temple that bears your Name and will cry out to you in our distress, and you will hear us and save us" (2 Chronicles 20: 6, 9 NIV).

I believe that David and Jesus did not encounter distress from fear, because this would suggest that David and Jesus doubted God's ability to save them from their circumstances. I have learned to call this distress *pressure*. The pressure caused by the reality of David's and Jesus's circumstances created distress, the normal stress associated with the reality of their circumstances. We falter in our faith walk with Christ when we allow the normal stress, pressure, or distress that comes with the reality of misfortune, injustice, and grief to invade our souls and wreak havoc with our thoughts and emotions, creating unnecessary stress that affects us spiritually, physically, emotionally, mentally, financially, professionally, and relationally.

Though distressed, David expressed his confidence in God's faithfulness to save him and rescue him from his circumstances. Psalms 57, 59, and 142 are associated with this season in the cave and Saul's pursuit of David. Jesus mentioned His distress in having to be the source of God's salvation for all humankind, but He understood that He would rise again and prevail against the sting of death and the power of the grave. How comforting it is to know that the Lord experienced distress! It helps me to understand Him as being fully human and fully divine. It teaches me to accept the reality of my own humanity in times of distress, understanding the privilege of having His divine nature and power within me to help and support me when I face dark times and difficult moments!

The principles of Christian fellowship, especially during times of distress, were played out during David's season in the cave and became a great source of spiritual encouragement and inspiration for me as I wrote this book. There are three specific types of fellowship that Christians should seek to incorporate in their faith walk with Christ in order to experience a balanced lifestyle as a believer: *private*, *public*, and *corporate* fellowship. Each type of fellowship is essential to the development of a believer who truly desires to grow as God requires for him to grow in Christ.

Private fellowship is the intimate time we spend alone with God in His word and in prayer. This kind of fellowship keeps us close and connected to Him as we seek to walk with Him by faith.

"In my distress I called to the LORD; I cried to my God for help. From his temple he heard my voice; my cry came before him, into his ears" (Psalm 18:6 NIV).

"Guide me in your truth and teach me, for you are God my Savior, and my hope is in you all day long" (Psalm 25:5 NIV).

"My heart says of you, 'Seek his face!' Your face, LORD, I will seek" (Psalm 27:8 NIV).

"I rise before dawn and cry for help; I have put my hope in your word" (Psalm 119:147 NIV).

Public fellowship is the time we share our faith with sincere believers, where we spend quality time sharing with one another what we believe, according to His word, about our circumstances. We disclose our personal struggles within trusted company to receive encouragement, support, and accountability.

"Let us not give up meeting together, as some are in the habit of doing, but let us encourage one another—and all the more as you see the Day approaching" (Hebrews 10:25 NIV).

"We proclaim to you what we have seen and heard, so that you also may have fellowship with us. And our fellowship is with the Father and with his Son, Jesus Christ" (1 John 1:3 NIV).

"Therefore confess your sins to each other and pray for each other so that you may be healed" (James 5:16a NIV).

Corporate fellowship is the time we come together in the sanctuary to worship God freely together in praise, prayer, and worship to receive from God the help He promises to send us from the sanctuary. Scripture supports each aspect of fellowship, and Christ's actions in the garden of Gethsemane endorse the necessity of fellowship, especially during the dark times and difficult moments of life when some may seek isolation and withdrawal as a means to cope.

"They devoted themselves to the apostles' teaching and to the fellowship, to the breaking of bread and to prayer. Everyone was filled with awe, and many wonders and miraculous signs were done by the apostles. All the believers were together and had everything in common. Every day they continued to meet together in the temple courts. They broke bread in their homes and ate together with glad and sincere hearts, praising God and enjoying the favor of all the people. And the Lord added to their number daily those who were being saved" (Acts 4:42–43, 46–47 NIV).

"Let the word of Christ dwell in you richly as you teach and admonish one another with all wisdom, and as you sing psalms, hymns, and spiritual songs with gratitude in your hearts to God" (Colossians 3:16 NIV).

In the face of great distress, internal pressure, and imminent danger, Christ modeled for us public and private fellowship. In contrast, His disciples portrayed the outcome of becoming overwhelmed with grief from distress and duress. In Matthew's gospel, we see an intimate encounter between Christ and three of his disciples—Peter, James, and John—that illustrates for us both private and public fellowship. Accounts in the gospels of Matthew, Mark, and Luke provide insight as to how and why the disciples handled the same circumstances of distress and duress that Christ faced. Their failure reinforces for us the necessity and value of prayer in the face of distress.

"Then Jesus went with his disciples to a placed called Gethsemane, and he said to them, 'Sit here while I go over there and pray.' He took Peter and the two sons of Zebedee along with him, and he began to be sorrowful and troubled. Then he said to them, 'My soul is overwhelmed with sorrow to the point of death. Stay here and keep watch with me.' Going a little farther, he fell with his face to the ground and prayed, 'My Father, if it is possible, may this cup be taken from me. Yet not as I will, but as you will'" (Matthew 26:36–39 NIV).

"When he came back, he again found them sleeping, because their eyes were heavy" (Matthew 26:43 NIV).

"When he came back, he again found them sleeping, because their eyes were heavy. They did not know what to say to him" (Mark 14:40 NIV).

"When he rose from prayer and went back to the disciples, he found them asleep, exhausted from sorrow. 'Why are you sleeping?' he asked them. 'Get up and pray so that you will not fall into temptation'" (Luke 22:45–46 NIV).

As we see in these passages, Jesus pulled aside three of his devoted followers and began to talk openly and transparently about the overwhelming sorrow He felt because of what He was facing. Matthew's gospel describes Jesus as being sorrowful and troubled. Mark's gospel describes Jesus as deeply distressed and troubled. Christ modeled public fellowship by initiating this intimate moment with His disciples, disclosing the reality of His humanity in the context of His current circumstances. The soul of our Savior was on display so that we can identify with the humanity of Christ, the intense suffering of His soul, and the intimacy of His ability to identify with our weaknesses because of what He suffered. This depiction of Christ is illustrated in both Hebrews 4 and 5 of the New Testament.

"For we do not have a high priest who is unable to sympathize with our weaknesses, but we have one who has been tempted in every way, just as we are—yet was without sin. Let us then approach the throne of grace with confidence, so that we may receive mercy and find grace to help us in our time of need" (Hebrews 4:15–16 NIV).

"During the days of Jesus's life on earth, he offered up prayers and petitions with loud cries and tears to the one who could save him from death, and he was heard because of his reverent submission. Although he was a son, he learned obedience from what he suffered" (Hebrews 5:7–8 NIV).

The life of Jesus Christ on earth teaches me two eternal truths. First, suffering was part of the plan of the fulfillment of salvation through Christ's crucifixion and resurrection. Second, Christ's life models for me how to endure, overcome, and push back against the seasons of misfortune, loss, and injustice associated with suffering. If suffering was included in God's plan for the life of His Son, the Christ, then I should not be surprised when I encounter suffering during my faith walk with Him. Continued reflection upon the truth of scripture, and study of David's season spent in the cave, have taught me that we never consider suffering in our desire to be blessed or in God's plan to bless us and bring us fulfillment. Despite the opposition and temptation Jesus faced in His mission to experience the fulfillment of salvation by dying on the cross, Jesus was resolute, passionate, and determined to fulfill His destiny.

It is God's desire that we allow the Spirit of Christ, who succeeded in His mission, to become manifest in and through us to experience the fullness of life that Christ came to give us. The one who was resolute, passionate, and determined about doing God's will now lives within us, through faith. He breathes the inspiration of God's word into our souls so that we may have our being in and through Him to live successfully and victoriously.

Insight reveals to me that the people who came to meet David at the cave were divinely sent by God's sovereign hand to support him in that season of his life. They were a response to David's prayers and a demonstration of God's love to aid and support David in his time of need. Though the people were described as being discontented, in debt, and distressed, their presence and support of David became a source of strength and encouragement that enabled David to escape the threat of death that pursued him and to fulfill God's destiny for him.

Regarding the subject of discontentment, I have encountered two essential truths. The moment I begin to sense the feelings and thoughts associated with dissatisfaction, I need to distance myself from them. And if I fail to accomplish this task, I will be overtaken by a negative attitude associated with being dissatisfied and discontented. Before long, this negative attitude will lead to feelings and thoughts of ingratitude, disenchantment, disenfranchised, depression, and defeat—along with feeling distant from God. In the same way that I would take action to improve the quality of my external, temporal life, I must seek to invest time, energy, and action in addressing the internal challenges that wrestle against my soul and inhibit or prohibit me from experiencing the fullness of life that Christ came to give me.

"But I have stilled and quieted my soul; like a weaned child with its mother, like a weaned child is my soul within me" (Psalm 131:2 NIV).

"The path of life leads upward for the wise to keep him from going down to the grave" (Proverbs 15:24 NIV).

"Remember your word to your servant, for you have given me hope" (Psalm 119:49 NIV).

"I was pushed back and about to fall, but the LORD helped me" (Psalm 118:13 NIV).

I am learning, as I walk with God by faith, that I must push back in the Spirit, with prayer, hope, perseverance, persistence, and an undeterred resolve that will propel me toward the fullness of life that Christ came to give me. The moment I sense myself being pulled away from wise, upward progress on the path of life, I know that is my warning signal to address what's happening internally, so as to keep me from being weighed down with chains of depression, dissatisfaction, and discontentedness. I must recall God's promises, reflect upon His goodness expressed to me in times past, and rejoice with assurance and confidence that God has the power to do what He promised!

As I learn to take action and to speak with the authority of His name and His word to quiet my soul and still the internal storms that rage within, I experience the anointing of His Spirit, which helps me walk in His peace—a peace that passes all understanding—until He makes the rough places smooth and the darkness light before me!

CHAPTER 6

MY WEAKNESS IS CHRIST'S POWER: GOD'S POWER THROUGH SALVATION

I want to know Christ and the power of his resurrection and the fellowship of sharing in his sufferings, becoming like him in his death, and so, somehow, to attain to the resurrection from the dead.

—Philippians 3:10–11

But you will receive power when the Holy Spirit comes on you: and you will be my witnesses in Jerusalem, and in all Judea and Samaria, and to the ends of the earth.

—Acts 1:8

In the preceding chapter, I attempted to share my insights about the outcome of a life devoted to the discovery and experience of God's promise of redemption and salvation through faith in Jesus Christ. To me, God's intention for fulfillment through salvation is a twofold experience.

First, salvation restores man's relationship with the Creator of the heavens and the earth, whereby man is provided privileged access directly to God, through Christ, to experience an intimate, personal relationship with Him.

Second, salvation authorizes and guarantees man's justification in God's sight. God freely pardons man from all offenses inherent in his sinful nature and offers to humankind the gracious gift of eternal life. This is God's great expression of love to those who believe and confess Jesus Christ as God's Son and accept Christ's death on the cross as the atoning sacrifice for man's sin. This recognition and acknowledgment of what Christ accomplished provides for man's redemption and his access into God's kingdom, including residence in the eternal home of heaven, which I refer to as the "glory of salvation." In the final two chapters of this book, I will share with you God's *power* and *glory* through salvation.

I believe that our understanding of God's power and glory in salvation are critical to our ability to experience them in our lives as we walk by faith in Jesus Christ. "Now to him who is able to do immeasurably more than all we ask or imagine, according to his power that is at work within us" (Ephesians 3:20 NIV). "No eye has seen, no ear has heard, no mind has conceived what God has prepared for those who love him" (1 Corinthians 2:9 NIV).

After salvation, what does God intend for us to experience? What does the Bible say about the life outcome of a person who accepts and believes in Jesus Christ, the Son of God, as Lord and Savior?

In the recorded history of the Bible, there was a group of people who initially believed and confessed that Jesus Christ was the Son of God and the Lord and Savior of their lives. After Christ's resurrection from the dead, these believers were misled into believing that they needed to practice the old Jewish ceremony of circumcision that had been required by God before Christ's death and resurrection. These believers had been told that circumcision was necessary to justify their right to eternal life and to assure their salvation. Perhaps they accepted this belief because they did not really understand who Jesus was or the significance of His death on the cross.

Because of this confusion, the apostle Paul was moved to write a God-inspired letter to the Galatians: "For if righteousness could be gained through the law, Christ died for nothing!" (Galatians 2:21b). "Neither circumcision nor uncircumcision means anything: what counts is a new creation" (Galatians 6:15 NIV).

The purpose of Paul's letter to believers was to remind them of the significance of their faith in Christ, whose finished work on the cross provides the grace, freedom, and power to experience God's promise of restoration. The book of Galatians enables believers to learn to live a life free of codes, laws, and rules implemented by men—regarded as *works*—to justify their salvation. This was necessary to keep believers from relying on a belief system that weakened the power of their faith in God through Jesus Christ. Paul saw that believers were being misled into thinking that Christ's completed work on the cross was insufficient to assure humankind's salvation. People were adding to their faith a system of actions, or works, to ensure their salvation.

This life of works, taught by men, is not the life God intended for us to live. It depends on human effort to justify some type of favor or acceptance from God. This kind of thinking or religion enslaves men into keeping a mental account of their good and bad deeds. If their bad deeds begin to outweigh their good ones, then they come up short, and God won't accept them. A life like this is dependent on human ability to consistently do good, hoping that God will be pleased with the effort.

This puts God in a position of constant judgment over us, and we see Him as someone who is demanding and very hard to please. It is difficult for us to perceive Him as someone who cares about us apart from what we do. Life becomes ritualistic and arduous, as we strain to feel loved, valued, accepted, and appreciated by a God who expects much from us but doesn't help us do what he requires of us. Eventually we realize that our human power is insufficient to do all that is required, and we can only hope that our works are sufficient. Our solace and satisfaction may only be in knowing that we're doing better than some other people. If *they* happen to be accepted by God in the end, then we should be fine. But what about those who are doing better than us?

Does this sound like a life lived with fulfillment, hope, peace, joy, love, and intimacy with the Creator of the heavens and the earth—the one whose Word promises that He will never leave us or forsake us and that He will come to us, live with us, and help us live for Him?

The life God desires for us begins with a simple act of faith. Christ's death and resurrection compel us to live for God, as Christ lives in and through us. God Himself provides us with the power to live in the manner He desires, according to His word. It is a life that does not require any effort, action, ability, or power on our part to gain it. We cannot and do not do anything to earn salvation from God as some sort of favor or acceptance from Him.

"For it is by grace you have been saved, through faith—and this not from yourselves, it is the gift of God—not by works, so that no one can boast" (Ephesians 2:8 NIV).

Salvation is freely given to anyone who believes in Jesus Christ and accepts His accomplishment on the cross as the atoning sacrifice for his sins. The believer then receives God's mercy, grace, acceptance, and the gift of eternal life. After receiving salvation, we then receive God's power. His Spirit lives in us, working along with our efforts to live the life He intended for us to live, according to His word. This is the power God uses to restore us to His image and likeness.

"For in Christ neither circumcision nor uncircumcision has any value. The only thing that counts is faith expressing itself through love" (Galatians 5:6 NIV).

God's power is available to those who believe in Jesus Christ and trust in God's word to fulfill what He promises and perform what He has said He will do. The first fulfillment achieved through salvation, according to what I understand about God's purpose in salvation, is to provide us with a source of power or ability that we did not have prior to our expression of faith in Jesus Christ. This is not a natural power or ability derived from within us, and we cannot access or activate it through positive thinking, meditation, or force of will.

"But as many as received him, to them gave he power to become the sons of God, even to them that believe on his name" (John 1:12 KJV). If we cannot receive this power through human will or natural ability, it has to come from a different source, a spiritual source: God Himself. It is accessed by faith in Christ as God's Son. This power activates a spiritual transformation and a connection with God as our Father. It changes the nature of my relationship with God from one of Creator and creature to Father and child.

"All these who believe this are reborn—not a physical rebirth resulting from human passion or plan—but from the will of God" (John 1:13 TLB). "Jesus answered and said unto him, 'Verily, verily I say unto thee. Except a man be born again, he cannot see the kingdom of God. That which is born of the flesh is flesh; and that which is born of the Spirit is spirit'" (John 3:3, 6 KJV).

If it were possible to accomplish God's plans for humankind's redemption and salvation without God, then I agree with the apostle Paul's conclusion stated in Galatians 2:21—that Christ died for nothing. The distinction between our human power and the power we receive from God helps me to understand two important truths. First, it was God's intention from the beginning for us to experience or access the power He provides for us to become sons of God. Second, just as Eve should have sought God for wisdom—and as Solomon did—God desires that we seek Him for the truth about this power that He freely provides for us. God does not desire that we be deceived, like Eve, or be misled into believing that we can earn God's favor by our own merit or works.

God showed us through the lives of Adam and Eve that He wants us to choose to live for Him in the way He intended us to live. Before they committed the actual sin of eating the fruit, Adam and Eve, by their actions, demonstrated their inability to live as God intended. With the power they had received from God, they chose the opposite of what He desired for them. I believe God wanted us to see—through Adam and Eve and through our own lives—that He never intended for us to live apart from Him or His truth that guides and governs our lives. We were not intended to exist in our own strength apart from His power, grace, and goodness. Satan's great deception since the garden of Eden has been to influence as many people as possible to make Eve's choice and rely upon *self*, without God or His help. More importantly, God wants us to reflect His image and likeness in our lives. All that He requires is that we choose to live for Him through faith in Christ.

Imagine, for a moment, that you have the ability to speak into existence the thoughts, ideas, and plans you have in your mind.

"In the beginning God created the heavens and the earth. And God said, 'Let there be light,' and there was light" (Genesis 1:1, 3 NIV).

Believe it or not, by being created in God's image and likeness, we share in the same creative ability or power that God displayed at the time of creation. "The tongue has the power of life and death, and those who love it will eat its fruit" (Proverbs 18:21 NIV). God has blessed us with the ability to speak into existence life or death, light or darkness, hope or despair. We have been given the privilege of using God's creative power to reproduce His image and likeness in the earth. Consider what God said about humankind's ability in Genesis 11.

> Now the whole world had one language and a common speech. Then they said, "Come, let us build ourselves a city, with a tower that reaches to the heavens, so that we may make a name for ourselves and not be scattered over the

face of the whole earth." But the Lord came down to see the city and the tower that the men were building. The Lord said, "If as one people speaking the same language they have begun to do this, then nothing they plan to do will be impossible for them." So the Lord scattered them from there over all the earth, and they stopped building the city." (Genesis 11:4–6, 8 NIV)

With the ability God had given them, humankind began to do, create, and build. People spoke into existence the plans, thoughts, and ideas they had in their minds. The problem with this story is twofold: (1) man desired to build a tower to the heavens to make a name for himself, not to glorify God, and (2) man did not intend to continue to fill the earth as God had commanded. Just as Adam and Eve had demonstrated in the garden of Eden, humankind continued to show an inability to live as God directed them. Instead they tried to live in a manner that brought glory, honor, and recognition to themselves rather than God.

In this scripture passage, God acknowledged clearly that humankind had the ability to accomplish whatever he set his mind to. History has proven this. Technology, transportation, and scientific achievements, as well as political and social movements, have changed the course of history for good. It is also clear that we often fail to do what God intends, or we are motivated by personal glory rather than God's.

This does not change the fact that God has given us natural power or ability to live in this existence. "You may say to yourself, 'My power and the strength of my hands have produced this wealth for me.' But remember the Lord your God, for it is he who gives you the ability to produce wealth" (Deuteronomy 8:17–18a NIV). In the book of Genesis, God declared that humankind should operate and function on earth with the same power, ability, and authority that He does.

"So God created man in His own image, in the image of God he created him; male and female he created them. God blessed them and said to them, 'Be fruitful and increase in number; fill the earth and subdue it. Rule over the fish of the sea and the birds of the air and every living creature that moves on the ground'" (Genesis 1:27–28).

"The highest heavens belong to the Lord, but the earth he has given to man" (Psalm 115:16).

"This, then, is how you should pray: 'Our Father in heaven, hallowed be your name, your kingdom come, your will be done on earth as it is in heaven'" (Matthew 6:9–10).

It was God's intention from the beginning that humankind live in the same manner, image, or likeness as His. God desires that we imitate Him, live as He lives, and do what He does. In my personal understanding of Psalm 115:16, I imagine God coming to me and saying, "If you want to experience on earth what I've promise in My Word, then you have to be willing to seek Me and pray and live according to my Word. Then you will see me, and I will reign in your life on earth as I do in heaven." This is how we experience God's kingdom power on earth—as it is in heaven. This process cannot begin, however, if we do not acknowledge Christ as God's Son, so that we can receive the power from God to live on earth as He does in heaven.

"Jesus answered, 'I am the way and the truth and the life. No one comes to the Father except through me'" (John 14:6 NIV).

"And He said to them, 'I tell you the truth, some who are standing here will not taste death before they see the kingdom of God come with power'" (Mark 9:1 NIV). Prior to making this statement, Christ had predicted his death and resurrection and had proclaimed to His disciples and the crowd gathered around Him what one must do to become a follower of Christ.

> Then he began to tell them about the terrible things he would suffer, and that he would be rejected by the elders and the Chief Priests and the other Jewish leaders—and

be killed, and that he would rise again three days after-
wards. Then he called his disciples and the crowds to come
over and listen. "If any of you wants to be my follower,"
he told them, "you must put aside your own pleasures and
shoulder your cross, and follow me closely. If you insist
on saving your life, you will lose it. Only those who throw
away their lives for my sake and for the sake of the Good
News will ever know what it means to really live. And
how does a man benefit if he gains the whole world and
loses his soul in the process? For is anything worth more
than his soul? And anyone who is ashamed of me and my
message in these days of unbelief and sin, I, the Messiah,
will be ashamed of him when I return in the glory of my
Father, with the holy angels." (Mark 8:31, 34–38 TLB)

After Christ's prediction of His death and resurrection, and
before His proclamation about living a life as a follower of Christ,
Peter hastily tried to stop Jesus from talking about His inevitable
suffering and persecution. Never mind the fact that Peter had
missed altogether Jesus's claim that He would rise again. I guess
Peter found it hard to imagine living without Christ's presence
in his life to comfort him and give him hope for living every day.
Peter had been a fisherman when he'd met Christ, but now he
had experienced the brief joy and personal privilege of seeing,
touching, and hearing the Master of the universe, who ate, drank,
walked, and dwelled with him. He had seen Jesus give light, life,
and hope to so many.

It was understandably hard and discomforting for Peter to
hear that this man of light would be extinguished. It was difficult
to bear the reality that this man who had given hope to so many
would be vanquished. He who had brought forth life with His
words and healed with a touch was to be killed. Such a thing was
hard for Peter to even imagine, and it was equally difficult to hear
what Jesus was saying. Peter decided that if it were up to him,
Jesus was not going to talk about such nonsense.

"He spoke plainly about this, and Peter took him aside and began to rebuke him. But when Jesus turned and looked at his disciples, he rebuked Peter. 'Get behind me, Satan!' he said. 'You do not have in mind the things of God, but the things of men'" (Mark 8:32–33 NIV).

Jesus recognized Peter's rebuke as the same temptation that Eve had experienced in the garden of Eden. It was the same temptation that men faced when they chose to build a tower for their own glory instead of God's and refused to spread out and fill the earth as God had commanded (Genesis 11). Peter's words spoke against what His heavenly Father desired for Him, and behind those words Jesus saw the influence of Satan trying to deceive Him into choosing the opposite of what God desired for His life.

Seizing the opportunity of a teachable moment, Jesus used Peter's words to make a clear and significant distinction, to His disciples and the crowd that had gathered, between living a life surrendered to Christ and a life of futility apart from Christ. After rebuking Peter, Jesus explained to the crowd that there was both profit and power gained by making the choice to follow Christ. He made it clear that if He desired what Peter desired for Him, then He would not desire what God wanted for His life—the redemption and salvation of humankind.

"This righteousness from God comes through faith in Jesus Christ to all who believe. There is no difference, for all have sinned and fall short of the glory of God and are justified freely by his grace through the redemption that came by Christ Jesus. God presented him as a sacrifice of atonement, through faith in his blood. He did this to demonstrate his justice, because in his forbearance he had left the sins committed beforehand unpunished" (Romans 3:22–24 NIV).

"For the wages of sin is death, but the gift of God is eternal life in Christ Jesus our Lord" (Romans 6:23 NIV).

In other words, Jesus was saying, "Peter, what you want me to do is not what God wants me to do. You want me to live for myself, to save myself and do what I want. My Father wants me to live for Him, to deny myself and my desires and do what He wants me to do. If I do what you want, Peter, there will be no power from God, through His Son, for humankind to live. Because of the penalty required for your sins, your accomplishments in this life will profit you nothing in the end.

"For whoever wants to save his life will lose it, but whoever loses his life for me and for the gospel will save it. What good is it for a man to gain the whole world, yet forfeit his soul? Or what can a man give in exchange for his soul?" (Mark 8:35–37 NIV).

In essence, Jesus was proclaiming His and the Father's purpose for everyone who believed Him to be the Son of God. He was saying that He had been sent by God to die for them so that they, through faith in Him, might live for God as He did. In the same way that Christ came and lived a life of sacrifice and service for the redemption and salvation of humankind, so God, in return for His love, desires that we live a life of sacrifice and service in Christ's name for God's glory.

In Mark 9, Jesus stated that some of the people who were standing with Him would not taste death before they saw the kingdom of God come with power. I believe He was referring to His resurrection. If you follow the sequence of His statements, they begin with His prediction of His death and resurrection. Second, He proclaimed the principles one must follow to become a follower of Christ. Third, He explained the profit or benefit of choosing to follow Him over rejecting Him, and He promised power to all who saw and received the truth He would later reveal through his own resurrection.

The only one in the crowd who would not be privileged to witness Christ's resurrection from the grave—that we are aware of—was Judas Iscariot, the disciple who chose to reject and betray Jesus. We discover in John 13:21–30 that Satan entered into Judas's heart and influenced him to betray Jesus. How could this be? Judas had walked with Jesus for three years! He had seen the miracles, heard the Master's voice, and witnessed countless miracles and testimonies from others about the power of God and salvation through Jesus Christ! How could Judas betray Jesus?

Judas had been surrounded by the presence and glory of God's power in his life. He had witnessed it and heard about it. He had even shared it with others when Christ commanded that His disciples go out in His name and authority to cast out demons and to teach the message of truth to others. The only place in Judas's life where he had not experienced God's power was where it mattered most. Surrounded by all that power and glory, Judas never allowed it to touch his heart.

We can be in a church building, surrounded by saints, hearing the unadulterated truth of the gospel and the majesty of the choir singing songs of triumph and victory. We can even share words of encouragement, enlightenment, and hope with others that empower them and give them life. But unless our hearts have been touched by the eternal truth of an internal belief in an eternal Savior, then we are lost eternally—like Judas.

"If I speak in the tongues of men and of angels, but have not love, I am only a resounding gong or a clanging cymbal. If I have the gift of prophecy and can fathom all mysteries and all knowledge, and if I have a faith that can move mountains, but have not love, I am nothing. If I give all that I possess to the poor and surrender my body to the flames, but have not love, I gain nothing" (1 Corinthians 13:1–3 NIV).

In all that Judas possessed and experienced in his life, he did not have the one, true possession that matters most in living a life filled with the fulfillment that God desires for us. Judas did not have the love of God, through Jesus Christ, in his heart. Judas had heard about it, seen it, and even experienced it to some degree in his life and the lives of those around him who testified about Jesus. He never, however, had that intimate, personal encounter with Christ that would allow him to experience true fulfillment and the life to come that Christ promised. Judas committed suicide two days before Christ rose from the dead.

"When Judas, who had betrayed him, saw that Jesus was condemned, he was seized with remorse and returned the thirty silver coins to the chief priests and the elders. 'I have sinned,' he said, 'for I have betrayed innocent blood.' So Judas threw the money into the temple and left. Then he went away and hanged himself" (Matthew 27:3–4a, 5 NIV).

After betraying Jesus, Judas could not live with the horror and shame of his sin. What is remarkable about this story is that Judas acknowledged and confessed his sin openly, but the burden and guilt of his sin was more than he could bear on his own, and he suffocated under the weight of his own guilt. In two days, he would have heard the good news about the risen Savior, His Lord Jesus Christ, and he could have received full pardon for the penalty of his sin and his failure. His failure, in God's sight, was no worse than the sins the other disciples had committed against Christ, for the Bible teaches that all have sinned and fallen short of God's grace.

Maybe the thought of having to face the other disciples after betraying Jesus right in front of them was an overbearing weight that Judas could not carry on his own. What he had done was unforgivable, wasn't it? In two days, Judas would have known the all-surpassing power of God's love to restore, redeem, and convert those would come to Him and receive forgiveness for their sins. This same Savior would pardon the sins of a thief, who admitted to being justly condemned for his sins as he died on the cross next to Jesus. He recognized Christ as his Savior and the Lord over all creation. Why would anyone, including Judas, not be offered the same pardon?

Don't be like Judas and suffocate under the weight of your guilt, shame, and failures. Turn to God, by faith in Jesus Christ. Believe in His promised forgiveness for your sins, and receive His eternal love offering of salvation.

When faced with the reality of suffering persecution for being associated with Jesus, Peter denied, three times, even knowing Jesus! This was the same Peter who had vowed that he would die for Jesus and would never deny Him, even if everyone else did. "Peter replied, 'Even if all fall away on account of you, I never will. Even if I have to die with you, I will never disown you.' And all the other disciples said the same" (Matthew 26:33, 35 NIV).

All the other disciples mentioned in Matthew 26:35 would include Judas. They abandoned Jesus after Judas betrayed Christ at His arrest in the company of the other disciples. This occurred after they all had vowed that they would never fall away from Him. Before Jesus's arrest, many people honored and praised His name when He entered the city of Jerusalem. But after His arrest, many of that same crowd mocked, scorned, and assaulted Him and demanded that He be crucified.

However, the weight of Judas's sin was more than he could bear. He did not have the strength, ability, or power to save himself from the internal suffering of his soul, and only two days before Christ's resurrection from the dead, Judas committed suicide. He missed out on the opportunity for his own personal salvation and redemption from his sins. Notice that *none* of the disciples had the power, ability, or strength to keep their promises to demonstrate their loyalty to Jesus.

After Christ's resurrection, Peter and the other ten disciples were restored in their relationship with Christ, even after abandoning Him. We see in the book of Acts that they were converted to preach the gospel as Christ's apostles, and countless others in the crowd had a change of heart after hearing the good news of Christ's resurrection from the dead. In one day, more than three thousand people committed their lives to Jesus Christ through the preaching of the apostle Peter, recorded in Acts 2:1–41! No doubt, the weight of Judas' guilt and shame in handing an innocent man over to death would be enough to debilitate anyone.

During the events in Jerusalem before the resurrection, Judas, the crowds, and even the disciples fell short of God's grace and were held accountable for their abandonment of Jesus Christ. They were insufficient in themselves to live out their faith and loyalty to Christ in the face of adversity and persecution. Unbelief, greed, and lack of foresight did them all in!

Judas had been part of the crowd when Jesus rebuked Peter and predicted His own death and resurrection. Judas had heard Jesus's proclamation about the profit and power provided to all who believed in Him and were willing to follow Him. What did Judas think when he heard this? Did he believe what Jesus was saying? Was he even paying attention to what Jesus was saying? Maybe Peter's comments distracted Judas from receiving, by faith, what Christ had proclaimed. Maybe Peter had caused Judas to doubt. Maybe Judas, like Peter, couldn't bear to hear about Jesus dying, which caused him to miss the part about Christ rising again after three days.

Maybe Judas felt that everything he had done for Jesus was in vain. Maybe he was deceived into thinking that his sacrifice to follow Him had been unfruitful. Maybe he thought that in return for following Jesus, he would only be alone again, unfulfilled in life. He would be without Jesus's comfort and presence. He would never be a primary benefactor when the Messiah took His rightful place as ruler over Israel. After all, Judas was one of Jesus's chosen disciples. Perhaps he felt he deserved more than this talk about giving up his own pleasures to live for Him. Jesus talked about dying, suffering, and persecution! Why was Judas following him? Was he devoting his life to continually sacrificing his life and desires for Jesus? But what about Judas? What did he get out of this?

When anyone hears the message about the kingdom and does not understand it, the evil one comes and snatches away what was sown in his heart. This is the seed sown along the path. The one who received the seed that fell on rocky places is the man who hears the word and at once receives it with joy. But since he has no root, he lasts only a short time. When trouble or persecution comes because of the word, he quickly falls away. The one who received the seed that fell among the thorns is the man who hears the word, but the worries of this life and the deceitfulness of wealth choke it, making it unfruitful." (Matthew 13:19–22 NIV)

Who knows what Judas was thinking? We do know that it is not God's intention for us to taste death without knowing, seeing, and experiencing for ourselves the intimate, personal power of God expressed through the death and resurrection of His Son, Jesus Christ. God desires for us to choose a life of surrender that will allow Christ to be formed in and through us. He wants us to live for Him and express His image and likeness in the earth. God chose humankind as the object of His affection, through whom He would express His eternal love. He chose to afford us the privilege of knowing that love intimately through His Son, Jesus Christ.

Don't allow yourself to experience a life of utter shame, disgrace, and unfulfillment as Judas did. Judas would have been privileged to the same mercy and grace God afforded to Peter, who denied even knowing Christ. God is willing to offer His love to you and to anyone who is willing to accept Jesus as Savior and believe that He is the Son of God who shed His blood for humankind's redemption and the salvation of their souls. Judas gave up two days before He could have received the grace, freedom, and power from God to live for Him and make amends for his failure.

Don't let Satan enter your heart and influence you to continue to reject the message of truth about Christ's death and resurrection and His proclamation about how to become a follower of Jesus Christ. Believe in His promise to give you power to live for Him and to tell others about His love, grace, and mercy that overcome the troubles, tragedies, and trials you have experienced in your life!

Trust in Christ as your Savior, and set Him apart as Lord in your heart. He will give you a personal, intimate understanding about His love for you and His desire to help you live for Him and through Him in this life! There is nothing in your past that God's love and power are unable to set you free from. Christ came to set you free, and when you know the truth, the truth will set you free. Whomever the Son of Man sets free is free indeed! There is nothing too hard for God, and what is impossible for you is possible with God. His arms are not too short to save anyone who desires to be delivered from a life of sin and rebellion, influenced by Satan. All that He requires is that we believe in Him as the only true God and His Son, Jesus Christ, as the One He sent for our redemption and salvation.

"For this people's heart has become calloused; they hardly hear with their ears, and they have closed their eyes. Otherwise they might see with their eyes, hear with their ears, understand with their hearts and turn, and I would heal them" (Matthew 13:15 NIV).

I encourage you to take a moment right now and simply ask God to open your heart to receive the Lord Jesus Christ. Confess with your mouth that you believe He is God's Son, who shed His blood on the cross for your sins. Ask God to help you to know and experience this personal, intimate life through faith in Jesus Christ, so you can begin to share His love with others as you grow in the love He has for you.

If you prayed this prayer and invited the Lord Jesus Christ into your heart, He is now with you, by faith. He will begin to reveal Himself to you and speak to you, to help you and guide you into all truth. I encourage you to begin reading a Bible that you can understand, and pray for understanding. Pray that the Lord will bring you into the company of people who enjoy talking about Jesus and their personal faith walk with Him, so you can learn more about His love and truth. If you are not currently attending church, pray that the Lord will guide you to a church that will help you learn and grow in His word and will encourage you to live for Him. Pray about all of these things, and ask for the Lord's guidance and direction, and He will help you.

This is the power God wants us to have through salvation. He empowers us to live for Him through faith in Jesus Christ. Our faith in Christ enables us to access God's power and help, and it gives us the ability to live the life He intended for us—a life that reflects His image and likeness in the earth, a life lived through the person of Jesus Christ.

"He is the image of the invisible God" (Colossians 1:15a NIV).

"The Son is the radiance of God's glory and the exact representation of his being" (Hebrews 1:3a NIV).

Through Christ, we see God. As we live by faith, Christ is expressed through us to others. God wants to express himself through you! Are you willing to surrender yourself to Him and allow Him to live in you and through you as Jesus did? Jesus lived for God and died for us so that we could experience the privilege and pleasure of God living in and through us by faith in Jesus Christ. Christ was raised from the dead so that we may know the full, complete power of God's love in the redemption and salvation of humankind. Because Jesus lives, we too will live with Him and reign with Him forever, if we believe in Him. Believe in the One God sent, and you will know the power of His resurrection!

CHAPTER 7

ELEVATED, EXPANDED, AND EXPONENTIAL LIVING: GOD'S GLORY IN SALVATION

In my Father's house are many rooms; if it were not so, I would have told you. I am going there to prepare a place for you. And if I go and prepare a place for you, I will come back and take you to be with me that you also may be where I am.

—John 14:2–3 (NIV)

For the Lord himself will come down from heaven, with a loud command, with the voice of the archangel and with the trumpet call of God and the dead in Christ will rise first. After that, we who are still alive and are left will be caught up together with them in the clouds to meet the Lord in the air. And so we will be with the Lord forever.

—1 Thessalonians 4:16–17 (NIV)

As I prepared to record my thoughts and begin my initial draft of this chapter on the subject of God's glory in salvation, I felt compelled to stop! Without understanding why, that urge was soon replaced with a strong desire to know more about the subject of God's glory before I continued.

Since that time, I have gained a wealth of experiential knowledge that has deepened my understanding and opened the eyes of my heart to God in a manner I had not known prior to this journey. I have since discovered a broadening of my own understanding of Him, and enlightenment on the subject of God's glory beyond what I had originally intended to write about. From the fall of 2005 through the summer of 2007, I felt led by the Lord to discover a deeper, more intimate comprehension of God's glory. I would soon discover that God had more for me to know, and I am grateful for having taken the journey with Him.

My initial understanding of God's glory had more to do with a place in the future called *heaven*. Since that time, I have grown to know that God's glory is more than a place in the future. It is also a manifestation of His person, presence, and power in this present world. I have grown to understand that God desires that we experience His glory now, while we are alive in this world, not just in a future heavenly world.

Moses understood this concept, because he asked God to show him His glory.

> The Lord would speak to Moses face to face, as a man speaks with his friend. Moses said to the Lord, "You have been telling me, 'Lead these people,' but you have not let me know whom you will send with me. You have said, 'I know you by name and you have found favor with me.' If you are pleased with me, teach me your ways so I may know you and continue to find favor with you. Remember that this nation is your people." The Lord replied, "My Presence will go with you, and I will give you rest." Then Moses said to him, "If your Presence does not go with us, do not send us up from here. How will anyone know that you are pleased with me and with your people unless you

go with us? What else will distinguish me and your people from all the other people on the face of the earth?" And the Lord said to Moses, "I will do the very thing you have asked, because I am pleased with you and I know you by name." Then Moses said, "Now show me your glory." And the Lord said, "I will cause all my goodness to pass in front of you, and I will proclaim my name, the Lord in your presence. I will have mercy on whom I will have mercy, and I will have compassion on whom I will have compassion. But," he said, "you cannot see my face, for no one may see me and live." (Exodus 33:11a–20 NIV)

The relationship Moses shared with God is one I believe God desires to have with all who profess faith in Christ, but not everyone seeks to experience Him as He desires to reveal Himself and make Himself known to us. God wants to express Himself to us intimately, personally, privately, and publicly, so that we may know, believe, and understand that He is and that He rewards everyone who diligently seeks to know Him as He desires to be known.

Did you catch Moses's request for God to show him His glory? Did you notice God's response? God referred to "all of His goodness" passing before Moses, the proclamation of His name in Moses' presence (personal revelation of God to Moses), and His mercy and compassion. God then took Moses to a private place and revealed Himself to him by allowing him to see His backside. God honored Moses's request to reveal His glory.

"Then the Lord said, 'There is a place near me where you may stand on a rock. When my glory passes by, I will put you in a cleft in the rock and cover you with my hand until I have passed by. Then I will remove my hand and you will see my back; but my face must not be seen'" (Exodus 33:21–23 NIV).

As you reflect upon these verses in Exodus, consider Moses's conversation with God before he requested to see God's glory. Moses (1) asked God to teach him God's ways so that he would know God, (2) desired that God's presence go with him, (3) sought to be distinguished as different from everyone else on earth as one who belonged to God, (4) demonstrated concern for God's people by requesting that the Lord be present with them to distinguish them, and (5) desired that God be pleased with him. This is an excellent biblical model of the *elevated*, *expanded*, and *exponential* living principles presented in this chapter.

Moses understood his position with God as he walked with Him. God allowed Moses to experience the elevated thinking that would align his mind and heart with God's plans and purposes for him. It became Moses's desire to do God's will over his own. It was equally important to Moses that God be present with him wherever he went, and he had no desire to go anywhere that God would not go with him. Moses modeled for us an example of elevated living and its challenges.

The beauty of seeking to embrace this lifestyle or thinking, as I have been privileged to do, is in having the imminent, personal presence of God to lead, guide, and teach me, so that I may experience the personal manifestation of His glory on a day-to-day basis. At one time in my life, I was blind about having such a relationship with God, let alone being conscious of His glory all around me. Now, like Moses, I am sharing in the privileged experience of a personal, intimate friendship with God through faith in Jesus Christ, and God is causing His glory and His goodness to pass before me, day after day, in ways that help me to know Him, please Him, and continue to receive His favor.

God's glory is evident all around us every day, but we do not always recognize it or become enraptured by it. The glory of God is revealed in nature. God's glory is in the sunrise and the sunset. It is in the melodious chirping of the birds, the snowflake that gently falls in winter, the morning dew that covers the open fields, and the raindrops that fall from heaven.

God's glory is revealed through humankind in the smile of a stranger or friend. It is in the encouragement of a timely word spoken to strengthen us and urge us to keep the faith. The glory of

God is revealed in the comforting words that come to us during dark moments, when our days are difficult and no relief appears to be in sight. God's glory is in a hug or a random act of kindness. God's glory is revealed through science and technology. The glory of God can be found in books, music, art, dance, on the radio, on television, or in a movie. God's glory can be found in the moment that inspires us to do good and seek the greater good of others. God's glory is in the birth of a child. And though it may be difficult to imagine, we can see the glory of God revealed even in the midst of death. God's glory is also revealed through hardships, difficulties, and the disappointing moments of life that seek to discourage, depress, and defeat us.

As I was writing the previous chapters, I obtained further insight, knowledge, and understanding. Prior to writing this chapter, I sensed that the Lord wanted to show me His glory of salvation, so I could convey an experiential knowledge that was more personal than technical. It was an experience I will treasure. The insight I gained has truly changed my perspective of what it means to be a Christian and how I seek to live as His child. I will first share my initial intent in writing about God's glory in salvation, and then I will disclose the inspiration that helped me to gain a deeper appreciation and reverence for the subject of God's glory.

I believe God wants to influence and inspire us to seek change in our position, perspective, and priorities of life. He desires that we be inspired by His word and influenced by His Spirit to live out His plans and purposes in our lives. I believe this because the Bible teaches us that faith in Christ causes us to be seated in heavenly places, where Jesus sits at God's right hand, which is a change in *position*.

My view of life, perspective, thoughts, actions, and choices, and the manner by which I seek to live day to day, were at one time left to my own discretion with little thought or regard for God's viewpoint. I had no desire to please God or to consider whether anything I desired was okay with God. I came and went as I pleased, with the intent to please myself in what I sought to do. Any consciousness I had of God was solely in the recognition that He existed, but I did not have a personal understanding of His imminent presence or His desire for me to share in an intimate relationship with Him as a companion or friend.

I certainly had no concept of God as my heavenly Father, who was willing to watch over me, to lead, guide, and direct me, and to help me live victoriously through the challenges I would face in this life. I had a basic understanding early in life that God existed, but I was blind about the possibility of experiencing an intimate, personal relationship with Him. I was left with a worldly perspective about how to deal with life. My understanding and wisdom on how to deal with the challenges of life were based on the knowledge I obtained from this world.

The change in my position came with the understanding that I no longer seek to live according to the principles of this world but according to my new position as God's child in this world through faith in Jesus Christ. Learning to live from my new position in heavenly places challenges me to think differently about how I live. Living from the perspective and position of the heavenly place influences me to think about how I live daily and how it will affect God, me, others, my environment, and eventually my reward for how I lived on earth. My position allows me to obtain the future paradise that the Lord has prepared for me to live with Him. This is what I would call *elevated living*.

"Once you were alienated from God and were enemies in your minds because of your evil behavior. But now he has reconciled you by Christ's physical body through death to present you holy in his sight, without blemish and free from accusation" (Colossians 1:21–22 NIV).

"Since, then, you have been raised with Christ, set your hearts on things above, where Christ is seated at the right hand of God. Set your minds on things above, not on earthly things. For you died, and your life is now hidden with Christ in God. When

Christ, who is your life, appears, then you will also appear with him in glory" (Colossians 3:1–4 NIV).

"Praise be to the God and Father of our Lord Jesus Christ, who has blessed us in the heavenly realms with every spiritual blessing in Christ. For he chose us in him before the creation of the world to be holy and blameless in his sight" (Ephesians 1:3 NIV).

"I have been crucified with Christ and I no longer live, but Christ lives in me. The life I live in the body, I live by faith in the Son of God, who loved me and gave himself for me" (Galatians 2:20 NIV).

Elevated living means embracing the inspired understanding that you, as a believer in Christ, are intentional and determined about living from the recognition of your *heavenly* position. You are no longer content to live a life, or seek after one, that consistently falls short of the fulfillment and abundance Christ came for you to have! You actually begin to long for, seek after, and pray for God's will and His kingdom to manifest in your life *on earth* as it is in heaven, just as Moses did. It means that you are serious and sincere about seeking first God's kingdom and His righteousness, believing that He will supply all of your needs according to His riches in glory.

Elevated living is an authentic life. It embraces the realities of life, faces them, and then aspires to live above and beyond the momentary circumstances that beset and trouble us all. Elevated living is not predicated upon superficiality, super-spirituality, or overindulgence. It is a simple life, in the sense of being practical, prudent, disciplined, and wise, not continually driven by lust, greed, envy, coveting, emotion, or heavy reliance upon one's own intellect. Elevated living means that you are not seeking to keep up with the Joneses or striving to maintain the status quo. Elevated living is a lifestyle inspired by a personal walk with God, through faith in Jesus Christ, which aligns itself with the teachings, guidelines, and instruction of God's counsel found in His word. It is a lifestyle that seeks to remain within the framework, boundaries, and ordinances that God has established for His people, according to His word, so that we may encounter and experience the blessings, reward, and fulfillment that He seeks to endow us with for our obedience and reverence.

This type of lifestyle carries with it a fragrance that arouses and captures the hearts of others, inspiring them to seek this way of life. Keep in mind that it was Moses's desire that God's people be distinguished from everyone else on the earth! Moses wanted to be recognized as belonging to God by the way he lived, and he sought God for the instruction on how to live that way.

Elevated living is a lifestyle that requires faith, prayer, and a continual, consistent diet of scripture in order to be obtained and maintained. It requires faith, because it is a lifestyle dependent on the supernatural provision of God to maintain and sustain. We do not have the means within ourselves to live according to God's holy ordinances, nor do we have the ability to remain consistent without the intervention of God to guide and direct us. Through God's Holy Spirit, we have access to His characteristics—hope, love, peace, joy, self-control, patience, kindness, gentleness, meekness, and faithfulness—and an intimate, personal relationship with God through faith in Jesus Christ.

I have yet to find a location where I can go to get these things when I need them. I have yet to meet a person who is able to endow me with these "fruits of the Spirit" when I have need of them. The elevated lifestyle requires prayer and the use of God's word in order to be lived out, because Jesus said that it is a lifestyle that few find. In the New Testament, the book of 2 Peter says that everything we need for *life* and godliness comes through our knowledge of God. Our knowledge of God comes from His word.

"Enter through the narrow gate. For wide is the gate and broad is the road that leads to destruction, and many enter through it. But small is the gate and narrow the road that leads to life, and only a few find it" (Matthew 7:13–14 NIV).

"His divine power has given us everything we need for life and godliness through our knowledge of him who called us by his own glory and goodness. Through these he has given us his very great and precious promises so that through them you may participate in the divine nature and escape the corruption in the world caused by evil desires" (2 Peter 1:3–4 NIV).

If the elevated lifestyle is one that only a few find, that means it is not clearly evident to us and must be searched for. If I want to be successful in obtaining this lifestyle, why not seek after the one who promises to provide it? I believe that one of the many reasons that few people find this lifestyle is the fact that it is a lifestyle of self-denial, self-sacrifice, and selflessness, which often do not garner reward, recognition, or success to the degree the world promises or that we desire. I have learned that I can be a Christian, walking on the broad path with the wide gate, when I am not allowing my soul to be guided and directed by His word and His Spirit. When I seek God's kingdom and His righteousness first, the elevated lifestyle I aspire to live offers more to me than what this world has to offer. For many of us, this concept is hard to embrace, because we *see* what this world has to offer, and it usually offers more than what we currently possess.

However, everything this world offers is not what we really need, and there is more to life than what we can *see*. Even if we possess most or all of the things this world has to offer, without the indwelling, intimate personal relationship with the Father, we would eventually squander what we have, lose interest in it over something or someone else, or allow it to consume us and lose ourselves in the process of obtaining what we desire.

The elevated lifestyle is a conscious act of our will, a consistent choice to live for God according to the principles of His word. It is a lifestyle that promises success and prosperity, but it also comes with moments of disappointment, disillusionment, conflicts, challenges, obstacles, and adversities. The one constant and consistent theme of the elevated lifestyle is the comforting and reassuring presence, power, and person of God inhabiting the hearts of those who believe and seek to live this lifestyle. Even with all that the world offers, it cannot offer that! God created the world and everything in it, so if I possess God, I possess more than the world: I possess the power by which the world was created!

"I pray also that the eyes of your heart may be enlightened in order that you may know the hope to which he has called you, the riches of his glorious inheritance in the saints, and his incomparably great power for us who believe. That power is like the working of his mighty strength, which he exerted in Christ when he raised him from the dead and seated him at his right hand in the heavenly realms" (Ephesians 1:18–19 NIV).

"And God raised us up with Christ and seated us with him in the heavenly realms in Christ Jesus" (Ephesians 2:6 NIV).

Before we accepted what Christ accomplished by dying on the cross for our redemption and salvation, it was recorded in scripture that our former position indicated that we were enemies with God in our minds and were hostile toward Him.

"The mind of sinful man is death, but the mind controlled by the Spirit is life and peace; the sinful mind is hostile to God. It does not submit to God's law, nor can it do so" (Romans 8:6–7 NIV).

"Once you were alienated from God and were enemies in your minds because of your evil behavior" (Colossians 1:21 NIV).

Life experience teaches me that even after salvation I can still be at odds with God, or I can become His enemy in my mind when I am unwilling to obey His word. Even as a Christian, I sometimes become unyielding to the changes in lifestyle that He requires of me, changes that will promote the growth and maturity of an elevated lifestyle. I can still be an enemy in my mind after receiving salvation, because I still have thoughts, habits, past experiences, current attitudes, and internal and external forces that seek to influence me on a daily basis. Without a sincere, deliberate effort to surrender my heart and mind to the influence and inspiration of God's word and the person of His Holy Spirit,

I will consistently operate, in my mind, against the will of God for my life.

This is significant, because I can be a Christian in belief but still not experience the change in *position* that comes from putting into practice what I believe according to what the scripture teaches. I may not fully understand what is available to me from a biblical perspective, because I may not have learned to consistently seek the scriptures to know and understand what God desires for a believing Christian. It is also possible that I may still have a strong desire for the things that this world offers, and I may have no desire for what God offers beyond my spot in heaven. I may be seeking only earthly glory and temporal blessings and the satisfaction and pleasure that I can get right now.

For this chapter, I had initially intended to write mostly about the life that comes in eternity as the promise or fulfillment of salvation, the end when Christ returns to receive those who have placed their faith in what He accomplished on the cross. The glory of Christ's promised return and the rapture of His bride is a message of hope regarded as a *living hope* by the apostle Peter in the New Testament book of 1 Peter. The scriptures teach us to encourage each other with this message until the day when Christ returns. In particular, Hebrews and 1 Thessalonians witness to us about the promised return of our King and the glory that will be revealed in His coming. Romans and 2 Corinthians explain it like this:

"I consider that our present sufferings are not worth comparing with the glory that will be revealed in us. The creation waits in eager expectation for the sons of God to be revealed. We know that the whole creation has been groaning as in the pains of childbirth right up to the present time. Not only so, but we ourselves, who have the firstfruits of the Spirit, groan inwardly as we wait eagerly for our adoption as sons, the redemption of our bodies. For in this hope we were saved" (Romans 8:18–19, 22–24a NIV).

"Because we know that the one who raised the Lord Jesus from the dead will also raise us with Jesus and present us with you in His presence. Therefore we do not lose heart. Though outwardly we are wasting away, yet inwardly we are being renewed day by day. For our light and momentary troubles are achieving for us an eternal glory that far outweighs them all. So we fix our eyes not on what is seen, but on what is unseen. For what is seen is temporary, but what is unseen is eternal" (2 Corinthians 4:14, 16–18 NIV).

The Bible talks about the Holy Spirit being a deposit to us from God, by whom we are sealed, guaranteeing our salvation on the day of redemption. I not only see this as a message of hope but as a message of assurance, because the troubles of this life, which Jesus said we would have, can sometimes be so great that we begin to doubt, question, or reject this message, and we can revert to a state of hostility with God. Life's pain, frustration, disappointments, discouragement, and heartache can really test our resolve and shake the foundation of our faith.

I know this, not only from my own experience but from John the Baptist, Jesus's cousin, who experienced a momentary lapse in faith and needed reassurance about whether Jesus was who He said he was. In Luke 7, scripture reveals to us that John the Baptist's earthly ministry—which preached repentance and the coming of God's kingdom through the person of Jesus Christ—had come to a halt when he was imprisoned. He was awaiting execution for preaching judgment against King Herod, who had taken his brother's wife, Herodias, as his own (Luke 3 and Mark 6). When we are allowed to view John's circumstances from Luke's perspective, we see that John sent two of his disciples to question Jesus about the authenticity of His claim to be the Son of God.

"John's disciples told him about all these things. Calling two of them, he sent them to the Lord to ask, 'Are you the one who was to come, or should we expect someone else?' When the men came to Jesus, they said, 'John the Baptist sent us to you to ask,

"Are you the one who was to come, or should we expect someone else?"'" (Luke 7:18–20 NIV).

Scripture says that this man was born for the sole purpose of preaching repentance and the coming of our Lord Jesus, and yet he questioned the authenticity of Jesus's deity! John the Baptist, Jesus's cousin, publicly acknowledged Christ as the Lamb of God who had come to take away the sins of the world. That same John the Baptist—who had witnessed the Holy Spirit descend from heaven and anoint Jesus when John baptized Him in the Jordan, and who had heard the heavenly proclamation from God that Jesus was His Son—was now grasping for assurance and relief from the distress of his circumstances in being imprisoned. He actually questioned whether or not Jesus was the one who was to come. How could this be?

The troubles of life that Jesus said we would have can choke out the hope and faith in our hearts and cause us to doubt and turn away from the truth of God. John the Baptist, I believe, needed reassurance because of the current adversity he was facing. I believe that John needed to know that some kind of glory would be revealed because of the hope he had placed in Christ. He needed this assurance to offset the groaning of his soul in his current suffering.

If we are not careful to embrace the Spirit-controlled mind that God desires for us, the darkness of our circumstances and the closets of our past can wreak havoc in our present and deter us from a future of hope, prosperity, and peace. That *mind,* the Bible says, will be kept in perfect peace, if it is stayed on Him and trusts in Him.

"At that very time Jesus cured many who had diseases, sicknesses, and evil spirits, and gave sight to many who were blind. So he replied to the messengers, 'Go back and report to John what you have seen and heard. The blind receive sight, the lame walk, those who have leprosy are cured, the deaf hear, the dead are raised, and the good news is preached to the poor. Blessed is

the man who does not fall away on account of me'" (Luke 7:21–
23 NIV).

Jesus's response to these men in Luke 7 is the point at which
I transitioned from my initial discussion of God's glory in salvation to the revelation I received while preparing to write this
chapter. John the Baptist received Jesus's report, but he did not
experience a change in his circumstances. If John received in
his heart the message and testimony of who Jesus was, then his
perspective about his circumstances would have changed. Even
though John's circumstances hadn't changed, he was reassured of
his position in Christ, which guaranteed that, though he might
die from his circumstances, he would live and reign with Christ
forever. Although his body was imprisoned, his mind was not!

My circumstances may look bleak and the outcome may be
uncertain, but with the perspective of a heavenly place—elevated
living—I can do all things through Christ, who strengthens me!
I am more than a conqueror through Christ Jesus. I may be hard
pressed by my circumstances, but I am not crushed. My financial
circumstances may be perplexing, but I am not in despair. I may
be experiencing persecution for seeking to uphold His holiness at
home or at work, but He will not abandon me. Though I may feel
struck down by life's blows, I am not destroyed. Because He lives,
I will live. Greater is He that is in me than he that is in the world!

John said that he would have to decrease so that Christ might
increase, but saying it and experiencing it were altogether different. I believe that John needed reassurance to uphold and uplift
him in his current circumstances so that he could endure the
hardship and persevere through his duress and distress.

Our circumstances may not change. There was a man named
Lazarus in the Bible who remained homeless, covered with sores,
and destitute, but when he died, he rested in Abraham's bosom.
Jesus told a parable about Lazarus to remind His followers about
the significance of saving faith in Him and the reward, or outcome, for one who believes and embraces the elevated perspective
of life. Our circumstances do not change our position in Christ,

where we are seated with Him in heavenly places, but in order to experience the transition of our new position, we have to consistently and continually allow change in our perspectives about God, faith in Christ, and lifestyle.

I had said previously that God wants to change our position, perspective, and priorities so that we can experience His great and precious promises in this life and the one to come. Our change in *position* begins when we place saving faith in our Lord Jesus Christ. But in order to *experience* and benefit from this new position of being seated in heavenly places with Christ, we must be willing to embrace the perspective God wants us to have.

This *perspective,* or elevated living, is what I would refer to as a *spiritual* or *biblical* perspective of life. This means that I consistently look at life from God's perspective and seek to live life according to what His word requires of me. It is *elevated*, because it is a perspective that reaches far beyond my comprehension and requires faith in order for me to live this lifestyle. It cannot be reasoned or rationalized through my own intellect. The elevated lifestyle transcends the circumstances of the moment and uplifts my mind and heart to the place where God can take hold of me and uphold me in my circumstances. He causes His goodness, mercy, compassion, and glory to uplift me and keep me going!

"Since, then, you have been raised with Christ, set your hearts on things above, where Christ is seated at the right hand of God. Set your minds on things above, not on earthly things. For you died, and your life is now hidden with Christ in God. When Christ, who is your life, appears, then you also will appear with him in glory" (Colossians 3:1–4 NIV).

What I enjoy about reading this passage is the discovery that God desires for me to live *with Christ in Him*! This helps me to better understand why Christ said that few people find this life: it is not a lifestyle that many seek or desire. This verse even goes so far as to say that Christ *is* my life and that I have died. To me, this means that when Jesus died for me, He died and rose again so that He might live through me. This allows me to live through Him, by the person, presence, and power of God's Spirit, and I will then learn to live as Jesus did. As He died for me, I must now seek to live for Him. In desiring and seeking to live this life, I die to myself, and the part of me that desired to live apart from God becomes crucified, just as Christ was crucified for me.

In the first century, Saul—who was later called the apostle Paul—sought to persecute and murder Christians who were part of the early church after Christ's resurrection. He was ultimately transformed into a man who was passionate about the teaching and preaching of God's truth! Paul's miraculous transformation is recorded in the New Testament book of Acts. On the subject of elevated living and a change in perspective, Paul wrote to the Galatians: "I have been crucified with Christ and I no longer live, but Christ lives in me. The life I live in the body, I live by faith in the Son of God, who loved me and gave himself for me" (Galatians 2:20 NIV).

Too often we seek to live according to the physical, material means of this world, and we neglect the immaterial, spiritual means that God requires us to seek. Living only according to the material and physical is temporal and unfulfilling. It always leaves us wanting, seeking, lusting, coveting, envying, and craving more. The Bible refers to a perspective apart from God as a *sinful* or *natural* perspective that is contrary to the life God desires and requires of those who have faith in Christ. Living a sinful life does not require me to have faith, because I was already living this life prior to being awakened to the presence and power of God in the person of Jesus Christ.

"Those who live according to the sinful nature have their minds set on what that nature desires; but those who live in accordance with the Spirit have their minds set on what the Spirit desires. You, however, are controlled not by the sinful nature but by the Spirit, if the Spirit of God lives in you. And if the Spirit of him who raised Jesus from the dead is living in you, he who raised

Christ from the dead will also give life to your mortal bodies through his Spirit, who lives in you" (Romans 8:5, 9, 11 NIV).

I can have faith in Jesus Christ and still be stuck in the darkness of my circumstances. I can be bound by my closets and restrained from the life that God desires for me to experience prior to heaven. God's word reveals my position in Him and facilitates the perspective needed to obtain the life He desires for us, but it is possible for a person to be ignorant of this. According to Romans 8, such a life involves God living in me. God does not just want to *be* in us, preserving us until we get to heaven. God wants to *live* in us and through us so that we can experience His glory, which is in heaven, while we are still on earth! When our perspective is aligned with the heavenly realms and we sincerely seek to learn God's ways—as Moses sought to do—we will begin to experience what I call *expanded* living.

The proper perspective of elevated living is facilitated by the process known in the Bible as a "renewing of the mind." Experiencing a renewed mind is a continuous, lifelong process of allowing our hearts and minds to become saturated by the Word of God. God desires that we allow the transforming grace and power of His truth to renew our way of thinking and to align it with how He thinks.

"You were taught, with regard to your former way of life, to put off your old self, which is being corrupted by its deceitful desires; to be made new in the attitude of your minds; and to put on the new self, created to be like God in true righteousness and holiness" (Ephesians 4:22–24 NIV).

"Your attitude should be the same as that of Christ Jesus" (Philippians 2:5 NIV).

"Do not conform any longer to the pattern of this world, but be transformed by the renewing of your mind. Then you will be able to test and approve what God's will is—his good, pleasing and perfect will" (Romans 12:2 NIV).

God wants us to allow our thoughts, desires, ideas, plans, goals, dreams, and aspirations to become aligned with His will for us. Then He can begin to accomplish His plans and purposes in and through us for His glory, our good, and the good of others. I believe that God's glory—His attributes and character—is expressed through the person of Jesus Christ in the life of a Christian. I would call this *expanded* living. Jesus's reply to the men that John the Baptist sent to Him in Luke 7 supports the principles of expanded living.

"At that very time Jesus cured many who had diseases, sicknesses and evil spirits, and gave sight to many who were blind. So he replied to the messengers, 'Go back and report to John what you have seen and heard: The blind receive sight, the lame walk, those who have leprosy are cured, the deaf hear, the dead are raised, and the good news is preached to the poor. Blessed is the man who does not fall away on account of me" (Luke 7:21–23 NIV).

I believe that Jesus was essentially saying, "Tell John that God's glory is being revealed in and through Me as a sign of my deity as Lord. It is manifested to many so that they too may believe in Me and receive the glory my Father gave to me to share with them." I believe this because Jesus requested that His Father God glorify His name through Jesus. In John 12, God responded that He had done so and would do so again. I believe the glory that God said He would do again in the life of His Son was the demonstration of His power in the resurrection of Jesus Christ from the dead.

Jesus could easily have answered a simple yes to the question asked of Him by John's messengers, but to give hope and encouragement to John and to validate the authenticity of His own deity as Christ, Jesus sent word of his Father's glory at work in His life. He concluded by reminding John not to give up hope, despite his current suffering. John chose to live a life of surrender to the purposes and plan of God's will for His life by proclaiming the coming of Jesus Christ. At the end of John's life, Jesus reassured him that there was more glory yet to be revealed, beyond what John had seen and heard on earth.

John lived his life with the passion and purpose of fulfilling God's will for his life by preaching the good news of Jesus Christ. John lived with a heavenly perspective and elevated thinking that expanded his ability to be influential. The way he lived inspired many to repent and prepare their hearts for the kingdom of God through faith in Jesus Christ. The response of those who heard John's message of repentance and surrendered their hearts to God was a reflection of the *expanded living* that comes from living out God's priorities. It was the visible outcome of faith at work.

The more I am willing to identify and align myself with Christ and His teachings through elevated living, the more influential and inspirational my life should become in influencing others for Christ's sake, which is expanded living.

"Then Jesus came to them and said, 'All authority in heaven and on earth has been given to me. Therefore go and make disciples of all nations, baptizing them in the name of the Father and of the Son and of the Holy Spirit, and teaching them to obey everything I have commanded you" (Matthew 28:18–20 NIV).

"I am the vine, you are the branches. If a man remains in me and I in him, he will bear much fruit; apart from me you can do nothing. If you remain in me and my words remain in you, ask whatever you wish, and it will be given you. This is to my Father's glory, that you bear much fruit, showing yourselves to be my disciples" (John 15:5, 7–8).

We are commanded and commissioned to affect positive change within the environments where God places us, motivating others to thirst and hunger for the life we have in Christ. Jesus says it is to the glory of God the Father when we live in a way that inspires others to follow Christ's example, which is lived out through us.

I believe this is the purpose of life: to bring God glory by the way we live. The glory of salvation is not just a "hereafter" concept of a far-distant, future experience. The glory of salvation is the glory of God manifested daily in the way we live for Him, which brings the attention of others to the reality of His person,

His presence, and His power in Jesus Christ. This inspires others to allow the glory of God's salvation to become manifest in their lives too!

"Follow my example, as I follow the example of Christ" (1 Corinthians 11:1 NIV).

"Blessed is the man who does not walk in the counsel of the wicked or stand in the way of sinners or sit in the seat of mockers. But his delight is in the law of the Lord and on his law he meditates day and night. He is like a tree planted by the streams of water, which yields its fruit in season and whose leaf does not wither. Whatever he does prospers" (Psalm 1:1–3).

The true evidence of our walk with Christ is shown when others seek to follow the example of Christ demonstrated by us. In my home, among my family members, or in the workplace, is anyone being inspired to follow the person and principles of Jesus Christ because of me? Am I living in a way that makes people thirsty and hungry for the knowledge of God and His righteousness? In God's economy of life, does my level of spiritual influence outdistance my financial and material prosperity?

The answer to that last question will identify the priorities by which I seek to live for God, if I am sincerely seeking to live for God at all. If I am the only person benefiting from the material and spiritual prosperity of Christ's salvation wrought in me by faith, then I must question whether I am living an expanded lifestyle according to the Word of God. Am I using what God has blessed me with to advance His kingdom and His ministries, to support His children, and to save the souls of those He desires to live with Him forever? Am I investing my time and energy in hoarding, squandering, lusting, wanting, and longing, or am I sincerely invested in enhancing the lives of those around me as the Lord enhances me? Am I invested in giving generously to the church and people in need, loving my enemies, sharing with others what God has freely given to me, caring for and helping the less fortunate, praying with and for others, and being willing to risk my life, reputation, or status for the advancement of another?

This is the life that few find. It is a simple life that is not pub-
licized or recognized, but it is rewarding and fulfilling, and it is
approved by God as the life He desires us to live with Christ in
Him. It is a life that God promises to reward beyond anything we
could ever obtain in this world, if we are willing to embrace His
lifestyle. The expanded living principles explained in this chapter
are the direct outcome of the elevated living principles applied by
those who sincerely seek to live according to the Word of God.
As my mind is consistently allowed to elevate to the heavenly
place with God, He promises that the direct outcome of this act
will be the intimate experience of Christ's life in and through me.
This is how Jesus explained it to His disciples.

> Thomas said to him, "Lord, we don't know where you are
> going, so how can we know the way?" Jesus answered, "I
> am the way and the truth and the life. No one comes to
> the Father except through me. If you really knew me, you
> would know my Father as well. From now on you do know
> him and have seen him." Phillip said, "Lord show us the
> Father and that will be enough for us." Jesus answered,
> "Don't you even know me, Philip, even after I have been
> among you such a long time? Anyone who has seen me has
> seen the Father. How can you say, 'Show us the Father?'
> Don't you believe that I am in the Father, and that the
> Father is in me? Believe me when I say that I am in the
> Father and the Father is in me; or at least believe on the
> evidence of the miracles themselves. I tell you the truth,
> anyone who has faith in me will do what I have been
> doing." (John 14:5–10a, 11–12a NIV)

In this exchange, Philip was asking Jesus about the place called
"glory" that Jesus had mentioned at the beginning of the chapter,
when He said that He was going to prepare a place for them and
would return to take them there. Jesus answered Philip, saying
that He was the way to that place, and because the disciples had

been with Him and seen Him, they had also seen the invisible God, the Father who was in heaven.

Philip then asked Jesus to show them the Father, just as Moses had requested of God Himself. Jesus replied to Philip, "I am here with you in the flesh! I am physically present for you to see, touch, and talk with. How long have I been with you, Philip, and yet you have not seen me as I have revealed myself to you?"

How long have we resided on this earth, and we have yet to know the Lord in the way He has revealed Himself to us? Philip had walked with Jesus for over three years, but he was still in the dark about who God was to him. Jesus then used the same response He had provided to John the Baptist's disciples. He said, "If it is difficult for you to understand what I am saying about seeing God by seeing me, then at least consider what God has been doing through me in the form of miracles as testimony of His glory—His person, presence, and power—revealed in and through Me."

Then Jesus concluded this revelation by declaring that anyone who had faith in Him would do what He had done! Jesus was revealing to His disciples what their faith would ultimately do for them. He told Philip that his belief in what He was saying would empower him to do what Jesus had done.

Jesus shared this same concept with Mary and Martha, the sisters of Jesus's friend Lazarus, whom He raised from the dead. Martha was grieving that Lazarus had been dead for three days. His body was in a tomb and was already beginning to decay. Just before Jesus raised Lazarus from the dead, He spoke to Martha. "Then Jesus said, 'Did I not tell you that if you believed, you would see the glory of God?'" (John 11:40 NIV).

The concept of expanded living was confirmed by Jesus's instructions to His disciples after He rose from dead.

"He said to them, 'Go into all the world and preach the good news to all creation. Whoever believes and is baptized will be saved, but whoever does not believe will be condemned. And these signs will accompany those who believe: In my name they will drive out demons; they will speak in new tongues; they will pick up snakes with their hands; and when they drink deadly poison, it will not hurt them at all; they will place their hands on sick people, and they will get well" (Mark 16:15–18 NIV).

Here are the instructions Jesus gave to His disciples when He sent them out, and the signs that He said would follow:

1. You will share with others what I have made known to you. As the Father sent me, so I am sending you.
2. You will have authority over the dark forces of this world and the spiritual realm, to overcome and prevail against whatever seeks to overcome and prevail against you.
3. You will learn to speak boldly and courageously about the truth and share with others what I reveal to you in My Word. You will encourage, comfort, and strengthen others, and urge them to keep the faith and fight the good fight of faith.
4. You will experience God's divine protection to preserve your life and face life's challenges with hope and courage.
5. You will have compassion for others, a willingness to help, a sincerity to love, and genuine humility to serve others. These will allow others to see Me through you.

Expanded living is the direct result of elevated thinking or living. Faith in God invites us to experience the glory of God before we get to heaven. God does not just want us to experience the wonder of His glory in creation or created things. He desires that we have a consistent, personal encounter with the Creator of the heavens and the earth. He desires that our consistent, elevated living overflow into the way we live, which will inspire and influence others, and many will see His glory in the earth. As we consistently seek to live by the principles of elevated and expanded living, the result will be exponential living that consistently reproduced

God's glory. It will be manifested as I am willing to allow Him to express Himself in me and through me to others for His glory.

Jesus confirmed this principle through His discourse with the disciples in John 14 and 15. "The words I say to you are not just my own. Rather it is the Father, living in me, who is doing his work" (John 14:10b NIV). "I am the vine; you are the branches. If a man remains in me and I in him, he will bear much fruit; apart from me you can do nothing. If you remain in me and my words remain in you, ask whatever you wish, and it will be given you. This is to my Father's glory, that you bear much fruit, showing yourselves to be my disciples" (John 15:5, 7–8 NIV).

Jesus testified to His disciples that it was the Father who spoke through Him and accomplished the miracles they had seen Him perform. He reminded His disciples that it would be to the Father's glory if they, in like manner, allowed the Father to work through them as He had worked through Jesus. Like Moses's dialogue with God in Exodus 33, Jesus concluded His admonishment with a declaration to His disciples. He told them that bearing much fruit—exponential living—would distinguish them as followers of Christ. This exponential living principle is also found in Ephesians and Philippians and confirms what Jesus said to His disciples about God doing the work through Him.

"For we are God's workmanship, created in Christ Jesus to do good works, which God prepared in advance for us to do" (Ephesians 2:10 NIV).

"Therefore, my dear friends, as you have always obeyed—not only in my presence, but how much more in my absence—continue to work out your salvation with fear and trembling, for it is God who works in you to will and to act according to his good purpose" (Philippians 2:12–13 NIV).

Exponential living is the multiplied experience of the expanded living principle in the life of a believer. Jesus described it as "bearing much fruit." As I consistently elevate my thinking to the heavenly place where God resides, God promises to expand Himself in and through me to accomplish His work to inspire and influence others to do the same. My diligence in remaining consistent will produce a fruitful multiplicity of God's glory being revealed in and through me. God does not need me to glorify Himself around me, because He has already accomplished that through the work of creation. God desires to duplicate the manifestation of His person, presence, and power in and through me, in order that I may participate in the work of His glory as I allow Him to work in and through me.

Here is what God said through the prophet Isaiah and the apostle Paul about the glory of salvation:

"Everyone who is called by my name, whom I created for my glory, whom I formed and made. 'You are my witnesses,' declares the Lord, 'and my servant whom I have chosen, so that you may know and believe me and understand that I am he. Before me no god was formed, nor will there be one after me. I, even I, am the Lord, and apart from me there is no savior'" (Isaiah 43:7, 10–11 NIV).

"Now to him who is able to do immeasurably more than all we ask or imagine, according to his power that is at work within us, to him be glory in the church and in Christ Jesus throughout all generations, for ever and ever. Amen" (Ephesians 3:20 NIV).

God created us for His glory! We were created specifically to glorify God and to be used by Him to express His glory through us. God wants to do great things in and through us for His glory from generation through generation, but we have to be willing to allow His power to work in and through us. God desires to reveal Himself, and He wants to reveal Himself *through us*! The real question is this: "Is that what we want from God?"

If you don't believe that God desires to reveal Himself to us intimately, personally, privately, and publicly, then consider this discourse between Jesus and His disciples in John's gospel: "Whoever has my commands and obeys them, he is the one who loves me. He who loves me will be loved by my Father, and I too will love him and show myself to him. Then Judas (not Judas Iscariot) said, 'But Lord, why do you intend to show yourself to us and not to the world?' Jesus replied, 'If anyone loves me, he will obey my teaching. My Father will love him, and we will come to him and make our home with him'" (John 14:21–23 NIV).

In this discourse, Jesus identified who would experience the personal privilege of seeing God the Father. Only those who honored His word would receive the personal revelation of Jesus Christ and the indwelling person, presence, and power of God through His Holy Spirit. If you read this passage carefully, you will notice that Jesus never answered Judas's question directly as to why He would only reveal Himself to them and not to the world. Jesus answered indirectly by describing who would experience the personal revelation of God through Jesus Christ. Everyone does not desire to know God as He desires to reveal Himself. Even Philip did not see God during the three years that he walked with Jesus! Those who don't believe may witness God through creation or as a result of something God did. But those who believe witness the Creator and the reoccurring expression of who God is!

I want to conclude this chapter by revealing to you how God decided to make His glory known to me in an intimate way. He truly inspired and educated me as to the significance of His glory in salvation beyond heaven.

Previously we looked at Exodus 33, where Moses asked God to show him His glory. To make a long story short, God did as Moses requested and revealed Himself to Moses. He also told Moses that He would proclaim His name in Moses's presence and would cause all His goodness to pass before him.

After becoming a Christian in 1993, I later understood, through the reading of scripture, that teaching was a gift given to us by God to edify His people and to help us to grow in the grace and knowledge of Jesus Christ. Since I have come to understand this gift, I have seen many manifestations of God's glory being revealed in the lives of my students, as well as their parents and families.

In the fall of 2005, at the beginning of the school year, I was reunited with a student I had known since middle school, and we were privileged to work together again on the high school level. For a time, life had been very difficult for her, and when I was reunited with her some three years later, I could see that things were not a whole lot better. This student was still victimized by the personal closets that I had been made aware of during the middle school years. Her darkness was drowning out the light of Christ's love that had been sown in her heart during conversations we had shared about His grace and truth.

I had just begun writing my manuscript for this book in June of 2005, and by October I was preparing to write on the subject of God's glory in salvation. At that time, I felt a prompting to stop and wait. It was also around that time that I was reunited with this student.

One fateful day, I invited her mom to come in to talk with me. I wanted to address some recent conflicts that had been stirring up again between her daughter and another student with whom she had been in conflict since middle school. When the mother arrived at my office, she came in and made her way to the seat I had prepared for her. As she sat, I saw a woman who appeared to be weary, weak, and worn from the challenges of raising a child and the burden of fighting desperately to save her child from the ravages of teenage drama.

In that instant, my mind's eye saw the person of Jesus Christ being crucified on the cross. It was not a literal image, but it was illuminated in my mind by this mother's love, compassion, and presence in seeking to support and demonstrate care for her child, who was suffering and struggling to live.

From this image, I heard the voice of God begin to communicate to me about His glory, which is revealed in suffering. I'm not talking about suffering for the sake of suffering, as if by seeking suffering we are made righteous in God's eyes. I am referring to the serious sincerity of seeking to live a life of love and to be an imitator of God in the face of adversity. Jesus would explain it as being willing to deny yourself, take up your cross daily, and follow Him. I am talking about the "suffering" you feel when you truly seek to live a spiritual life from heaven's perspective, even when everything in you wants to do opposite. I am talking about a mother who had been through hell and back, seeking desperately to love her daughter through her child's prodigal season of life, when she could very easily have kicked her child out of her home and said good riddance!

I believe that God was talking to me about the glory of Jesus Christ revealed in this mother's acts of mercy, grace, and goodness toward her daughter, who was struggling to live the full, abundant life Christ had come to give her. This mother's love was covering a multitude of sins, and though it was painful to witness it, it was the exact representation of Christ's suffering—the glory of God's love expressed to humankind for our redemption and salvation. This mother's actions communicated to her daughter: *I am always with you. I will be by your side through thick and thin. I know it's rough right now, but we will get through this together. I will never leave you or forsake you.*

Through this brief encounter with this parent and her daughter, God began to reveal Himself to me through the subject of suffering as an expression of His glory. I was then led to Jesus's discourse with His Father in John 12. His request for the Father to glorify His name came at a moment when Jesus was expressing concern about being crucified, wondering whether he should ask to be saved from God's will by being spared from death. He encouraged Himself by saying no and reflecting on the fact that it was this very purpose for which He had come into the world. It was then that He asked His Father to glorify His name. Prior to this, Jesus had just healed a blind man and had raised his friend Lazarus from the dead. In both accounts, Jesus had concluded that the suffering of these two men—blindness, sickness, and death—existed so that His Father's glory might be revealed in and through Jesus.

You would have thought from what I just shared with you that the story of the mother and her daughter, along with Jesus's discourse in the gospel of John, would have been enough. But God was just warming up, and now that He had shown Himself to me, He was going to show off! About a year later in 2006, I was cosponsor of the Christian Youth Club at the high school where I work, and I was reacquainted with another student whom I had worked with in middle school. Little did I know that God had a plan to teach this student, her mom, and myself about His glory in salvation.

Not long after the school year got underway and the students began attending Christian Youth Club after school, I was leading one particular session and happened to mention something related to the subject of teenage pregnancy. This caught the attention of one of the students. She later confided in me that she was pregnant and thought I knew. I was amused at her belief in my ability to know her circumstances. I told her that I'd had no idea my message was convicting her, but through my message, God had prompted her to come forward so that He could help her with her pregnancy. I had no idea that my lesson that day and her disclosure were going to play a large role in all of us seeing God's glory revealed through these circumstances.

The student, her mother, and I began to take a faith walk together, which included prayer, home Bible study visits, and multiple conversations with the student to provide words of encouragement as they sought to have the child and continue to prepare for graduation. The journey was trying and difficult, but grace prevailed!

On one occasion, I was privileged to be informed that the mother had taken the week off from work, months into the pregnancy, to be at home with her daughter during an intense time of physical discomfort due to the pregnancy. This act of tenderness, compassion, and self-sacrifice for her daughter ministered to me about the act of love and grace that God provides for us—even when we are beset with circumstances that are the direct result of our own poor choices and sin. I was moved by this gracious act of a mother toward her daughter. I witnessed the power, person, and presence of God at work in the life of a mother and daughter, in the midst of trying circumstances, that enabled them to work through a very challenging season of hardship—all because a parent was willing to allow God to work in her to act according to His good purposes for the benefit of her daughter and His glory!

After graduation, I was privileged to assist the student in finding a place to move into, to begin the transition from high school graduate to adulthood and parenthood. This was truly one of the most rewarding moments in my life as a professional and a Christian. I had been an intimate participant, watching God glorify Himself through the life of this student and her family. I had shared in the experience of assisting this student during her pregnancy and as she started life as an adult after graduation. This is only one of many moments when I have been privileged to learn to allow Christ to work in me and through me for His glory. It was even more meaningful and rewarding, knowing that I was being led by God to be a witness of His glory in salvation!

CHAPTER 8

CONCLUSION: STEP INTO THE LIGHT

I will lead the blind by ways they have not known, along unfamiliar paths I will guide them; I will turn the darkness into light before them and make the rough places smooth. These are the things I will do; I will not forsake them.

—Isaiah 42:16 (NIV)

But you are a chosen people, a royal priesthood, a holy nation, a people belonging to God, that you may declare the praises of him who called you out of darkness into his wonderful light.

—1 Peter 2:9 (NIV)

During the summer of 2011, I encountered a personal, intimate revelation of God that inspired me to start a devotional writing ministry, and I began to share with the tenants of the apartment complex where I lived. The revelation that illuminated my heart and mind was "my Immanuel," which means "my God is with me."

"The virgin will be with child and will give birth to a son, and they will call him Immanuel—which means, 'God with us'" (Matthew 1:23 NIV).

Understanding that one of God's names is *Immanuel*, which means, "God with us," I was inspired to add the word *my* to God's name. This signified to me God's intimate and imminent presence with me during the most difficult and trying seasons of my life following separation and divorce. I received this revelation as God's intimate expression that He is with me, has been with me, and will continue to be with me as I strive to walk with Him by faith. The inspiration from the revelation, "my Immanuel," led to the 2011 production of a devotional ministry titled *His Intimate Imminence* and a 2012 blog on wordpress.com titled *My Immanuel.*

The mission behind the ministry was to share the inspired revelation that God is with others as He is with me. I wanted to relay God's proclamation and promise to be with those who believed, so that they might experience the comfort, encouragement, and hope in His word that had ministered to me. It was a profound revelation for me at the time, because I was struggling to maintain my sanity in the midst of an unsettling time in my life. I was facing the monthly ordeal of the threat of eviction, mounting financial problems, distress at work, and internal distress from gnawing thoughts and emotions that wrestled against my faith and hope in God to deliver me from all of my fears, cares, and anxieties.

The reality of my circumstances was too great for me to cope with on my own. I often expressed to God in prayer that I felt weak, weary, and worn. Journaling became a great source of comfort that provided consistent and continuous inspiration and helped me to progress through what I would often refer to in my journal as "difficult days and dark moments."

The words, thoughts, and feelings that were difficult to express verbally, I could easily put on paper. With the use of scripture, I documented my expressed desires, thoughts, and feelings to God that would help me to, as I said in my journal, "relinquish to God my distress so He could release me from my duress." Writing these things down enabled me to better express them verbally—

when I wasn't journaling and communicating with God in prayer. I always repeated aloud to God what I'd written on paper as a way to express what I thought and felt on the inside. I soon discovered that the journaling helped me to better identify what I was thinking and feeling and the source behind those thoughts and feelings.

The journaling also became a source of inspiration for declaring new seasons, a means to channel my focus toward the future instead of reliving the past or thinking that there was no hope for me. I said things like "moving forward and looking ahead." My current season was "my season of progress, success, and prosperity." Prior to this, I declared a season of empowerment and fulfillment that lasted over a year.

Journaling also became a great source of inspiration for insights, revelation, illumination, knowledge, and understanding, which I gained from reading God's word and reflecting upon what I was learning. God provided revelation and inspiration from His word, which led to my new devotional ministry. It also reminded me of a biblical character whose personal, intimate relationship with God inspired a ministry of revival in his community—just as God had inspired one through me. The story of Josiah in 2 Chronicles 34–35 is one of my favorite Old Testament stories. Josiah's life makes a connection with mine on a personal level because of the absence of his father and the way God used Josiah to inspire others.

The story of Josiah begins with the death of his father at the conclusion of 2 Chronicles 33. Josiah's father, Amon, son of Manasseh, began his reign as king at age twenty-two. His reign only lasted two years. Amon is described as one who did evil in the eyes of the Lord, just as his father, Manasseh, had done before him, but unlike Manasseh, Amon did not repent. Eventually, Amon was assassinated. The historical account of Amon's life, legacy, and reign as a king of Judah reads like a short obituary. My father was not murdered, but my memory of him is a brief encounter of two outings—bowling and horseback riding—and then he was gone.

Josiah was eight years old when he experienced the loss of his father. I was four years old. A product of separation and divorce as a child, I did not see or feel the loss of my father until, as an adult, I was transitioning through separation and divorce myself. As the father of two children, I now strive to remain engaged and invested in the lives of my children in a way that my father did not.

Recently, as my children were helping me to distribute one of my devotional writings, *His Intimate Imminence*, to the apartment complex where I once resided, we passed the apartment in which they had spent time with me. My son said to me, "We had a lot of fun in that apartment!" Though I was unable to remain married, I am blessed and fortunate to share in the lives of my children and to contribute to their childhood with positive memories of interacting with their dad—something I was unable to experience with my own father.

Later, during a conversation with my mother, I learned that my father's abandonment had been perpetuated by his own admission that he did not believe that my sister and I were his children. So, on top of abandoning the family, he had disowned his own flesh and blood. I said that my father, unlike Amon, was not murdered, but my relationship to my father was dead.

During the time I transitioned through the dark days and difficult moments of my own separation and divorce, I began to encounter grief associated with my childhood. As an adult, I grieved more about my childhood than I had done while growing up. Despite the tremendous disappointment in experiencing separation and divorce, I saw the fragmented family structure of my childhood continue into my adulthood. I consider myself both blessed and fortunate to have seen the many ways that God used my misfortune, injustice, and grief to touch, change, and transform others through the platforms He provided me to serve Him and others.

From 2001 to 2010, as an educator in Prince George's County Public Schools, I had the distinct privilege of working with adolescent youth and older adolescent young adults at the middle school and high school levels in a program called "Peer Mediation." Through the process of teaching and training students to help each other resolve peer-to-peer conflicts, God gave me the opportunity to be a minister of reconciliation for those who chose to confide in me. And their struggles provided healing for me too! In fact, my very first encounter with a student in my role as the peer mediation coordinator was to provide encouragement to a young man whose family was going through the transition of separation and divorce.

This helped me to understand what Isaiah prophesied, on the subject of fasting:

> Is not this the kind of fasting I have chosen: to loose the chains of injustice and untie the cords of the yoke, to set the oppressed free and break every yoke? Is it not to share your food with the hungry and to provide the poor wanderer with shelter—when you see the naked, to clothe him, and not to turn away from your own flesh and blood? Then your light will break forth like the dawn, and your healing will quickly appear; then your righteousness will go before you, and the glory of the LORD will be your rear guard. (Isaiah 58:6–8 NIV)

During that same season, from 2003 to the present, God also allowed me to serve as a co-facilitator for the nonprofit agency, The National Family Resiliency Center, formerly known as Children of Separation and Divorce. The organization focuses on providing information, encouragement, and coping strategies for families going through the transition of separation, divorce, and issues related to child custody. My childhood and adult experiences with separation and divorce have provided me with great insights to share with the families I encounter when I am a presenter for this organization. It has also been a great resource of encouragement and help for me. Throughout my childhood and adult life, God has been faithful to His promises to be with me, to never leave me nor forsake me, and to cause everything to work together for good.

This is the second reason that I identify with the life of Josiah. Not only do our lives mirror each other's in relation to the pain and grief of losing a father-son relationship during childhood, but we also experienced the power of a Father-child relationship with God as we transitioned into adulthood.

Being able to identify with the lives of those who were immortalized in the pages of scripture enables and empowers me to live with hope and expectancy that God will be with me and work in and through me, just as He did for them—because God is the same today, yesterday, and forever!

"For everything that was written in the past was written to teach us, so that through endurance and the encouragement of the Scriptures we might have hope" (Romans 15:4 NIV).

After Amon's death, Josiah began his reign as king at the age of eight. He ruled his nation for thirty-one years. Unlike his father, Josiah was described as one who did right in the eyes of the Lord—so much so that the Bible says that he walked in the ways of his father David, not turning aside to the right or to the left. Clearly, King David, the man who slew Goliath, was not Josiah's father, but Josiah came from the lineage of kings that was part of the fulfillment of God's covenant promise to David: "Your house and your kingdom will endure forever before me; your throne will be established forever" (2 Samuel 7:16 NIV). Josiah was a descendant of David. Jesus Christ, also a descendant of David and the King of Kings, was the fulfillment of God's covenant promise to David that his throne and kingdom would be established forever.

The loss of Josiah's father did not have to deter Josiah from experiencing an extraordinary life. Josiah chose to look beyond the limitations of his father's poor example and followed the example of his ancestor David as a model for how he would be king. "Josiah was eight years old when he became king, and he reigned in Jerusalem thirty-one years. He did what was right in the eyes of the LORD and walked in the ways of his father David, not turning to the right or to the left" (2 Chronicles 34:1–2 NIV).

During the time of his reign as king, Josiah made a decision to follow the example of his ancestor David, a man after God's own heart. This enabled and empowered Josiah to progress, succeed, and prosper in his role as king. In fact, Josiah encountered two significant transitions, which are highlighted in 2 Chronicles 34:3. It says there that Josiah, in the eighth year of his reign, at the age of sixteen, made a decision to seek the God of his father David. Unlike his father, Amon, Josiah chose to make the Lord his first priority. Amon, like his father, Manasseh, before him, had worshipped other gods and had never repented, setting a poor example as the leader of God's people. This led to his death by assassination.

Instead of allowing the life and legacy of his father to cripple him and prevent him from encountering the extraordinary blessings and fullness of life that God promised to those who kept His commandments, Josiah chose to blaze a new trail. Eight years into his reign, Josiah made a conscious decision to walk by faith. He transitioned from a past associated with loss, grief, and the death of his father and stepped into an extraordinary encounter in his faith walk with God.

"In the eighth year of his reign, while he was still young, he began to seek the God of his father David. In his twelfth year, he began to purge Judah and Jerusalem of high places, Asherah poles, carved idols and cast images" (2 Chronicles 34:3 NIV).

The second half of verse 3 says that Josiah, in the twelfth year of his reign as king, at age twenty, began to inspire revival by destroying the idols and images that distracted the people's focus from God. Josiah's personal faith relationship with God began to have a public impact in his environment. Josiah made use of his role and position as king to affect positive change in the world around him. From age sixteen to age twenty, Josiah had an extraordinary encounter with God that inspired an extraordinary outcome in the way he lived as an adult—four years after making the conscious choice to seek the God of his father David.

"Josiah removed all the detestable idols from all the territory belonging to the Israelites, and he had all who were present in Israel serve the Lord their God. As long as he lived, they did not fail to follow the Lord, the God of their fathers" (2 Chronicles 34:33 niv).

"The Passover had not been observed like this in Israel since the days of the prophet Samuel; and none of the kings of Israel had ever celebrated such a Passover as did Josiah, with the priests, the Levites and all Judah and Israel who were there with the people of Jerusalem. This Passover was celebrated in the eighteenth year of Josiah's reign" (2 Chronicles 35:18–19 niv).

In the eighteenth year of his reign, by age twenty-six, Josiah had successfully affected positive change through his role as king, which remained during the time he served as king. At age sixteen, Josiah chose to seek the kingdom of God and His righteousness, and by age twenty-six, Josiah encountered the fulfillment of being devoted to God. His private devotion to God blossomed into a public and professional worship lifestyle that inspired revival.

Josiah's life reminds us that no matter what our childhood was like, sincere devotion to God, at any age, will allow us to step into the fullness of life that Christ came to give us. When we read the account of Josiah's life carefully, we discover that he distinguished himself and influenced others in a way that preserved his life and legacy like no other king of Israel, including David. As He did with Josiah, God wants to do something in and through us that will distinguish us as His children and allow us to encounter His extraordinary power, which will empower us to live extraordinary lives.

Despite the abuse, abandonment, rejection, isolation, misfortune, and grief I've encountered, God is continually showing me His salvation. As I walk by faith, I continue to encounter the extraordinary redemptive, regenerative power of His Holy Spirit, who is at work in and through me as I step into the light of His grace and truth through every age and stage of development in life. From humble beginnings—the fourth of four children and a product of a divorced household—God compelled me to step into the light of Jesus Christ. This has led to me serving as a facilitator to help families experience success through the transition of separation, divorce, and child custody!

God wants to use you to inspire revival in others, just as He used Josiah! As He produces revival in you to be conformed to the image of His Son, Jesus Christ, God invites you to share with others your extraordinary encounter with Him.

"When they saw the courage of Peter and John and realized that they were unschooled, ordinary men, they were astonished and they took note that these men had been with Jesus" (Acts 4:13 NIV).

No matter what your past mistakes are, what your childhood was like, or how difficult are your current dark moments, God still has something extraordinary in store for you—if you believe Him and step into the light.

Peter denied that he knew Jesus Christ, even after walking with Him for three years. John deserted Jesus in the garden of Gethsemane after declaring that he would not betray Jesus. Despite their misdeeds, God restored them, empowered them with His Holy Spirit, and led them to inspire revival in the hearts of many, just as Josiah affected change in his generation. Their influence continues to this day.

As Josiah patterned his life after David's, I have been inspired by the Rev. Dr. Martin Luther King Jr. I envisioned myself in a better place, even as I transitioned through the process of grief and loss associated with separation and divorce as an adult. Faith in Christ has revealed to me that where my earthly father was insufficient in his role and responsibility, I have a heavenly Father who will never leave me or forsake me, a Father who will bless me to live an extraordinary life as I walk with Him by faith!

Peter, John, and Josiah all shared something in common: their personal devotion to God and their faith in Jesus Christ led them to encounter extraordinary lives that influenced revival in others. It was said of David, "For when David had served God's purpose in his own generation, he fell asleep" (Acts 13:36 NIV). My sincere prayer is that it will be said of me what was said of David.

Salvation is the extraordinary encounter with God that transforms us as we experience our faith walk with Him, making the world around us a better place in the process. It's time to step into the light to encounter the extraordinary!